'It's so beautiful round here, isn't it?'

'Mmm,' Lucas murmured, with a faster beating pulse as his glance took in the slender stem of her neck rising smooth and sun-kissed. *He'd* been hurt in mind and body, he thought, but Jenna was beautiful and untouched—which was how it should be.

She was observing him with questioning eyes above the sparkling liquid in the glass and, twirling the stem of it between her fingers, she commented, 'You're miles away.'

He shook his head. She was wrong. He was exactly where he wanted to be.

Dear Reader

Welcome to the first of my books where coast and countryside combine to bring you the beautiful Devon village of Bluebell Cove. A place where doctors and nurses in the medical practice look after the health of the local folk and share their joys and sorrows, and in return have the respect and support of their patients when it is their turn to need a friend.

I live in a village in the Cheshire countryside myself, and it never ceases to amaze me how close is the bond between those who live here. When one of them hurts they all hurt. When one of them rejoices they all rejoice.

In WEDDING BELLS FOR THE VILLAGE NURSE a bubbly young nurse finds the man of her dreams in Bluebell Cove. But not without first having to break through barriers created by disillusion and disenchantment.

If you have enjoyed reading about the folks there, do look out for their stories in books two, three and four. They'll be coming along shortly.

So do let's keep in touch, dear reader, as I write and you read about golden beaches, clotted cream teas, and *romance* in Devon— glorious Devon!

Abigail Gordon

WEDDING BELLS FOR THE VILLAGE NURSE

BY
ABIGAIL GORDON

First published in Great Britain 2010
Large Print edition 2010
Harlequin Mills & Boon Limited,
Eton House, 18-24 Paradise Road,
Richmond, Surrey TW9 1SR

© Abigail Gordon 2010

ISBN: 978 0 263 21123 8

Printed and bound in Great Britain
by CPI Antony Rowe, Chippenham, Wiltshire

Abigail Gordon loves to write about the fascinating combination of medicine and romance from her home in a Cheshire village. She is active in local affairs, and is even called upon to write the script for the annual village pantomime! Her eldest son is a hospital manager, and helps with all her medical research. As part of a close-knit family, she treasures having two of her sons living close by, and the third one not too far away. This also gives her the added pleasure of being able to watch her delightful grandchildren growing up.

Recent titles by the same author:

COUNTRY MIDWIFE, CHRISTMAS BRIDE*
A SUMMER WEDDING AT WILLOWMERE*
A BABY FOR THE VILLAGE DOCTOR*
CHRISTMAS AT WILLOWMERE*
COUNTRY DOCTOR, SPRING BRIDE
A SINGLE DAD AT HEATHERMERE

The Willowmere Village Stories

For my niece Nicola
and her daughter Chloe,
far away in Texas

CHAPTER ONE

WHEN Jenna Balfour looked out of the window of the taxi as it cruised along the coast road on a Sunday afternoon in midsummer it was there down below, beautiful and changeless. A strip of golden sand where Atlantic breakers, white edged and powerful, forever staked their claim, and today, as was often the case, surfers were there to challenge them with boards at the ready.

It had been her favourite place while she'd been growing up and nothing had changed while she'd been studying nursing at a London college. Every time she'd been home on vacation she'd gone down to the beach to surf within minutes of arriving home.

But all that had changed. She hadn't seen the

house on the headland where she'd been brought up and the beach below for two years— ever since she'd insisted she wanted some time out to see the world before falling in with her mother's wishes for her to join the local practice that Barbara Balfour ran with brisk efficiency.

Her father had understood how Jenna had felt. A retired solicitor who'd had a practice in the nearby town, he was easy to talk to and treated his bubbly only daughter, who had eyes blue as the sea below and hair the colour of corn at harvest time, with a whimsical affection.

Her mother rarely had time for family discussions and preferred results to rhetoric. Both father and daughter had cause to think that the practice came first, family second, with her, and for the main part they accepted it in the knowledge that Barbara Balfour was held in high esteem by patients and staff alike.

Eventually there had been a row, a big one, with Keith Balfour in the middle trying to keep the peace between the wife and daughter he loved, but it hadn't worked and Jenna had gone to follow her dream in angry rebellion instead of with her mother's blessing.

She'd regretted it as soon as she'd gone, but her mother wasn't the only one with a mind of her own and she'd stayed away until the day that a phone call from her father had wiped out all the anger and she'd found herself getting an early flight home from the French town where she'd been doing some bank nursing.

He'd sometimes rung her for a chat, but his tone on that occasion had been serious, and she'd listened to what he had to say in shocked amazement. Her mother had been forced to take early retirement from the practice that was her life's blood because of severe rheumatoid arthritis.

'She needs two sticks to get around and it is difficult because her hands are so swollen. Sometimes we use a wheelchair,' he'd said.

There had been silence while Jenna had digested that and then she'd said slowly, 'Was this coming on when Mum was so keen for me to join the practice as soon as I'd qualified?'

'She'd seen a rheumatologist, yes, but wasn't expecting such a fast deterioration and now in spite of the fact that you quarrelled she needs you, Jenna, though she won't admit it.'

'Yes, of course,' she'd said immediately, thinking tearfully that her mother being the needy one would be a first. 'Give me a couple of days to sort things out at this end and I'll be with you as soon as I can.'

'Shall I tell your mother you're coming?'

'It's up to you, Dad. Do what you think best. She's never been keen on surprises, you know.'

'She'll like this one,' he'd promised reassuringly, and that had been it.

And now in a few moments she would be back in the place that was so dear to her heart. The countries she'd visited had been interesting. She wouldn't have wanted to miss the experience, but the grass wasn't always greener on the other side of the fence, she'd found. It had been more a case of her wanting to stretch her wings a little before returning to her beloved Devon.

There was no car on the drive when the taxi turned onto it and her heart missed a beat. Her dad knew she was coming even if her mother didn't, so where were they?

As she put her key in the lock of a front door that had weathered many a storm in its exposed position, the phone rang and when she picked it up her father's voice came over the line in a whisper.

'Ah, Jenna, you've arrived,' he breathed. 'I haven't told your mother you're coming home. I wanted it to be a complete surprise. When she suggested that we drive out into the countryside for a cream tea this afternoon I couldn't very well drop it on her at the last moment, knowing what a stickler she is for everything being cut and dried.

'We are in the tearooms now, waiting to be served. It's quite a long drive back, so it could be a couple of hours before we return, but it will at least give you time to get settled before the two of you meet.'

'Er yes, I suppose so,' she said weakly into the

anticlimax. 'I'll see you later, but what do we do if Mum doesn't want the joyful reunion bit?'

'I suggest we worry about that when it happens' were his parting words.

It had taken just a matter of minutes to make herself a coffee and a sandwich, then she went upstairs to unpack. As she crossed the landing the door of her parents' bedroom was open and they were all there, the aids to mobility that were the lifesavers of those who had very little of it.

How could it all have changed so suddenly? she thought dejectedly. Her mother had always seemed invincible, nothing ever pierced her armour of capability, but something had, a creeping painful illness that was attacking her freedom of movement and the amazing energy she'd always had.

In her own room, overlooking rocky cliffs that descended to the seashore, there was comfort to be had. It was exactly as she'd left it, with her surfboard propped up in the corner, and as she stroked it lovingly it seemed to be just the thing to take away the hurt of arriving to an empty house with so much worry on her mind.

A summer sun was beating down and the sea was so blue she gave in to temptation. Deciding there was no need for a wetsuit, she fished out a bikini and once she'd changed into it tucked a towel under her arm. With sandals on her feet she picked up the surfboard and after locking the door behind her began to walk down the road that led to the beach.

She usually clambered over the rocks as a more speedy way of descending but today, wanting to savour every moment of her return, she used the slower and more sedate pathway.

'Hi, Jenna, where've you been?' a male voice cried as she hit the beach. 'Haven't seen you in ages.'

It was Ronnie, one of the lifeguards out on patrol, and as he came loping across she laughed up at him, the reason for her being there forgotten in the pleasure of the moment.

He was a muscular thirty-six-year-old, married

with a wife and children he adored, living in a cottage at the other side of the bay, and always had a cheery greeting for Dr Balfour's daughter when she came surfing.

'I've been taking some time out,' she told him, 'and am now back for good.'

'Great!' he enthused. 'We've been short of glamour on the beach since you went.'

'Yes, I'll bet,' she joked, 'and where is everyone on a sunny day in the height of the holiday season?'

She'd seen a few surfers in the water when she'd been looking through the window of the taxi, but now there was only one and he was on the point of coming out, carrying his board as he strode towards them.

'They've all gone to the opening of a new theme park not far away,' he replied, 'or disappeared earlier on fishing trips.'

Out of the corner of her eye Jenna saw that the man who had just come striding out of the surf had stopped beside a folded towel and was now drying himself briskly. As she observed him she thought with a body like that he put Ronnie's bronzed biceps in the shade.

He was half-turned away from them and she registered a thatch of dark hair, flat and glistening wet against his head, and hands with long supple fingers holding the towel. The vivid scar that she'd noticed across his chest as he'd moved in their direction was no longer visible, but there had been time for her nurse's practised eye to observe that it was red and jagged as if from a recent injury.

'Not good about your ma, is it?' Ronnie was saying sympathetically.

'No,' she replied glumly, taking her glance off the man with the scar and feeling that until she'd seen her mother for herself she didn't want to talk about it.

'Cheer up, Jenna,' the amiable lifeguard said, sensing a drop in spirits. 'How about a kiss to celebrate your return?'

She was smiling again. Ronnie was a tease. 'You'll have to get down on your knees and beg,' she told him.

He obeyed with a bellow of laughter and, planting a butterfly kiss on the top of his head, Jenna left him there and began to move towards the water.

The solitary surfer had finished drying himself and as he turned to pick up his board they almost collided as they came face to face.

'Sorry,' he said abruptly.

'It's OK,' she told him easily, meeting the dark hazel gaze that was also part of the package with a sudden feeling of breathlessness and weakness of the knees.

He would be a tourist, she could bet on it, she was deciding, while at the same time registering that there was no responding cordiality in *his* expression. So with that thought in mind she sidestepped him and proceeded towards a joyful reunion with the pounding Atlantic breakers.

When she turned he'd gone and so had Ronnie. She had the beach to herself and in a moment of wild joy Jenna walked into the oncoming tide with surfboard at the ready.

She could have stayed there for ever, but a glance at her watch said that soon her parents would be back and the moment she was dreading would be upon her.

Had the young blonde in the bikini been the Balfours' prodigal daughter? Lucas Devereux pondered as, with feet slapping wetly against the stone of an old causeway, he walked to where he'd parked his car.

He'd heard the lifeguard greet her and the name had fitted, as had the flippancy she'd displayed. He'd wondered a few times how a daughter could leave her mother in the state that she had been in during her last months as head of the practice and flounce off to do her own thing.

Keith had been there for Barbara, of course, and he was much easier to get on with than his wife. She was a very strong character, while all her husband asked for was peace, and from what he'd heard the man didn't get much of that.

They'd met the other day in the post office and the retired solicitor had told him that their daughter was coming home, that it was going to be a surprise for her ailing mother, and he would be obliged if Lucas didn't mention it to anyone else.

He'd replied grimly that being involved in the affairs of others was not his forte, far from it, and that no one was going to get to know of Jenna Balfour's return from him. No doubt if it *had* been her on the beach they would find out soon enough. In the close community of Bluebell Cove news got around faster than the speed of light.

As he drove inland from the beach the white-washed wall of The Tides practice loomed up in front of him with its tubs of summer flowers at the entrance and a long wooden bench for those who preferred to wait their turn outside— weather permitting.

When he'd been discharged from the hospital where he'd been employed ever since qualify-ing and had ended up as a patient after an incident that had almost cost him his life, he had been persuaded by his friend Ethan Lomax to move into community health care work for a while in a coastal suburb of Devon that was blessed with golden sands and backed on to fertile countryside.

On doing so, he had rented a property called The Old Chart House just a few doors away from the surgery and it was there that he was heading with his expression just as sombre as it had been earlier when he'd seen the girl that he'd surmised might be the Balfours' daughter.

Just as that family were going through a sticky patch, so was he, and the only person who knew about that was Ethan, who had taken over as senior partner in the local practice when the re-doubtable Barbara had been forced to let someone else take the reins.

His friend had visited him in hospital a few times after the incident that had nearly killed him and had made him feel like turning his back on medicine for ever. He'd been perform-ing a routine operation, serious enough but not normally life threatening, when the patient, a woman in her thirties, had gone into shock and died almost immediately on the operating table. There had been no response to resuscitation and he'd had the unpleasant task of telling her husband the tragic news.

The man had gone crazy, his outrage outweighing his grief, and as Lucas was turning away he'd lunged at him with a knife that he'd produced from somewhere and slashed him across the chest. The thin hospital gown he had been wearing had been no protection and the wound was life threatening.

Afterwards, on several of his visits, Ethan had mentioned casually that there could be a place for him here in Bluebell Cove if he so desired, in quieter, less stressful surroundings than those of a big hospital.

At the time he hadn't been even remotely interested. The future had loomed like a black abyss with no sense or reason in it. But as his body had slowly healed he had accepted grimly that surgeons at the hospital where he saved lives had given him back his, and he was going to have to drag himself up out of the black void.

* * *

In the end he'd listened to what Ethan had to say with regard to life in a place like Bluebell Cove being lived at a slower pace, and his friend's comment that surgeons of his standing were few and far between when he'd said he was thinking of giving up medicine.

He'd taken indefinite leave from the hospital in the nearby town where he'd been the top cardiovascular surgeon for the past five years and so far it was working out all right because he had fallen completely under the spell of Bluebell Cove. So much so that he was in the process of buying The Old Chart House and turning part of it into a private heart clinic which would fill the time when he wasn't helping out at the surgery. But the nightmare that had brought him there still tormented him in the long hours of the night and on awakening.

On the outside he still gave off an aura of cool competence, but underneath there was hurt and disillusion and the fear that he would never again be the man who had always taken life by the horns, had known where he was going, what he was aiming for—that sort of confidence was now in short supply.

The one thing that his friend hadn't taken it upon himself to offer advice on was Lucas's broken engagement to Philippa Carswell, who had worked with him in the cardiac unit at Hunters Hill Hospital.

It had occurred just before the attack on him and he'd never mentioned it since, but there'd been a drawn, pinched look about him afterwards. At the time it had been thought by some that the broken engagement had affected his work and had led to the death of the patient on the operating table which had triggered off the savage attack on the hospital's top heart man.

But while Lucas had been fighting for his life enquiries had shown that as usual his work had been faultless, and that the demise of the woman undergoing heart surgery had been due to a massive embolism that had blocked the main pulmonary artery and caused sudden death.

* * *

Jenna was framed in the open doorway as her father helped her mother slowly and painfully out of the car. She wanted to run to her and hold her close, but caution was holding her back. They'd parted on bad terms, for one thing, and for another it was rare for her mother to be at a disadvantage in a situation. She doubted she would take kindly to this one—a gentle approach was called for.

When Barbara straightened up on the drive supported by the two sticks that Jenna's father had mentioned, she looked up and saw her, and Jenna felt her throat go dry as the moment took hold of the three of them.

Her mother's face was slack with surprise and the colour was draining from it as she said, 'Jenna! Where have *you* come from?'

'Just across the Channel, Mum,' she said softly as she walked towards her.

'Why didn't you let me know what was happening to you, for goodness' sake? I would never have gone if I'd known.'

Barbara's smile was wintry. 'I'm not used to

pleading. I couldn't use my fast-approaching immobility as a means of tying you to me.' She turned to her husband, who so far hadn't spoken. 'You are behind this, I suppose, Keith?'

'Yes,' he said stoutly, 'and don't tell me that you're not pleased.'

There was no reply forthcoming to that. Instead she asked Jenna, 'So how long are you here for?'

'As long as you need me. I'm home for good.'

Her mother's face was crumpling. 'Even though I'm still a bossy and cantankerous woman? I don't deserve you both.'

'We'll say hear, hear, to that, won't we, Jenna?' Keith joked, gazing at the two women in his life and smiling his relief.

One day he would tell Jenna what it was that had driven her mother through all the years when they and the practice had been in two very separate compartments of her life, theirs being the smaller. But in the meantime Barbara needed to be inside and resting after their drive across the downs on the cliff tops and into the countryside.

The sun was setting like crimson fire on the horizon as Jenna gazed down onto the beach later that evening. Her mother was asleep and her father contentedly watching television.

She had helped Barbara to undress and assisted with her toiletries, and when she had finally settled against the pillows her mother had taken her hand into her own swollen one and without any words of endearment had said simply, 'I will sleep better tonight not having to wonder where you are and if you're safe.'

Knowing that such a comment coming from her was the nearest she might ever get to 'I love you', Jenna had kissed her gently on the brow and said, 'Don't disturb Dad if you need help in the night. Call *me*, yes?'

'Yes,' her mother had replied obediently and they'd both dissolved into laughter at the reversal of their roles, and the moment of shared amusement was another first.

And now the night was still young and there were lots of folk on the beach and in the sea, out to enjoy every moment of the waning day. Ronnie must have been right, she decided. Their absence in the afternoon had been because there had been something special on.

'I'm going for a stroll,' she told her father on returning to the sitting room.

'Sure,' he said easily. 'I will most likely have gone to bed by the time you get back so I'll see you at breakfast, beautiful daughter.' With a twinkle in his eye, he added, 'I thought sometimes that you might bring the man of your dreams back with you one day.'

'No chance. I met one or two nice guys, but Mr Right wasn't amongst them. I think he's still on the drawing board,' she said lightly, and for a moment the man with the amazing attractiveness *and* closed expression that she'd seen on the beach came to mind.

There had been no mention of the practice since she'd arrived home, Jenna was thinking as she walked slowly along the road that led inland from the seashore, and when there was, what was she going to say?

There might be no need to say anything if the surgery was fully staffed, and how would she feel then—disappointed? That kind of thing was in Ethan Lomax's hands now. He was senior partner and would be the one she needed to talk to if she wanted to work there.

She'd always wanted a career in nursing and having had her time out was ready to put to use the skills and knowledge that she'd acquired during her training. Most of the friends she'd made during that time had gone into hospital situations but, Jenna thought whimsically, they hadn't had a mother who'd been the best G.P. for miles around and had wanted the same kind of dedication from her daughter.

The local pub was just a few doors away from the surgery and when it came into sight she saw that all the tables and chairs outside were occupied by those who had been tempted out by the mellow night.

Someone called across to her. She waved but didn't linger and carried on walking past the surgery towards The Old Chart House, which had been empty the last time she'd seen it.

A guy was cutting the lawns at the front of it with a powerful machine and even with his back to her she recognised the stance of him as the surfer she'd met that afternoon.

As the memory was taking shape he swung the mower round to face the front and it was as before, a meeting of glances.

'Hello, there,' he said. 'We met earlier on the beach, if I'm not mistaken.'

'Yes,' she replied, and having no wish to give the impression that she'd seen it as a memorable occasion commented, 'I'm surprised to find this place occupied. It has been empty for a long time.'

'So I believe,' he replied, resting his arms on the handle of the mower. 'I rented it originally, but when I decided to stick around I wanted living in Bluebell Cove to be a more permanent thing, and have heard only today that my purchase of the property has gone through.'

'Wow!' she exclaimed. 'It's a lovely house. Congratulations!'

'What for?' he asked dryly. 'Buying a house that is far too big for me?'

'So you live alone?'

'Yes, where do you live?' *As if he didn't know.*

'With my parents at the moment in the house on the headland called Four Winds.'

So he was right, Lucas was thinking. This *was* the Balfour girl, having changed the bikini for a blue cotton sundress that matched her eyes.

There might have been a time when he would have warmed to her attractions but after Philippa the mighty ocean not far away would freeze over before he made that mistake again. From what he'd heard this one had an eye to the main chance too, leaving her mother in the state she'd been in when he'd made the acquaintance of the staff at The Tides practice.

He had no family and envied those who had in whatever shape or form. His father had died while he'd been at medical school fifteen years ago, and as an only child he'd been very protective of his mother until she too had succumbed to inoperable cancer.

Philippa Carswell had been his second in command on the cardiology unit at Hunters Hill Hospital, with hair the colour of fire and the passion to go with it. He'd been in love with her and had believed she'd returned his feelings.

As well as being physically attracted to her, he'd admired her determination to get to the top of her profession, until he'd discovered that she had intended him to be a casualty on the way.

But she'd reckoned without friendship. He'd always had a good relationship with fifty-year-old Robert Dawson, head of the hospital trust at Hunters Hill, and one night when the two men had met up for a meal, which they did occasionally, his friend had warned Lucas that Philippa wanted his job and had told him that she would do *anything* to get it.

He might have doubted the truth of it coming from anyone else, but not from Robert, who was the soul of integrity. When he'd challenged her about it she'd laughed in his face and commented that all was fair in love and war.

It had been war all right from that moment on, and realising she'd gone a step too far she'd packed her bags and gone to work in America, leaving him with a jaundiced view of the opposite sex, beautiful ones in particular.

Discovering that he'd been just a rung on the ladder of her ambition had been the first life-shattering thing to happen to him, but the next had been far worse and he was always going to carry the scar from the stab wound he'd received that day.

It was one of the hazards of being a doctor, one he could have done without, but he'd forgiven the culprit and was trying to get on with his life in the slower, less fraught kind of way that Ethan had described by holding a twice-weekly heart clinic at the practice where the other man was in charge. He was also in-tending to open up a private consultancy shortly, in the house that was now his.

It was all very different from the life he'd envisaged for himself. With Philippa gone and the cut and thrust of the cardiac unit at the hospital no longer at his elbow all the time, whether he was going to be happy in it remained to be seen, but no doubt, as it always did, time would tell.

While his thoughts had been somewhere else Jenna had been observing him warily, keen to know who he was but not about to ask. She sensed something in his manner and as she'd never met him before until today it was strange. Her curiosity was increasing by the second.

It was not to be satisfied, however. He wasn't quite as aloof as when they'd met on the beach, but no name or any other item of information was forthcoming from him. Only one thing was sure, he'd bought The Old Chart House so she would be seeing him around and that was a thought not to be treated lightly.

'Bye for now,' she said breezily into the silence that had fallen between them. 'I hope you'll be happy in your new home.'

'Thanks,' he replied, taken aback at receiving

good wishes from a stranger, and as if he had to justify himself for some reason he went on, 'I'm not sure about that, but I do admit that I've fallen in love with this place, the house, the beach, and the green fields of Devon stretching as far as the eye can see.' His voice hardened. *'Those kinds of things don't change.'*

'Er, no,' she agreed, not sure what to make of that, and turning to go back the way she'd come, she left him with a casual wave of the hand.

When she'd gone he stood without moving, staring grimly into space. What on earth had possessed him to start chatting to her? If she was out to scrape an acquaintance she'd chosen the wrong man. He might have been a fool once, but twice? Never!

When she awoke early the next morning Jenna could already hear the laughter of children down below and the deeper tones of parents, signalling that the tide was out. Further along on the headland someone had lit a fire and she could smell bacon cooking.

If only her mother was in better health she would be content, she thought as she watched them from her window. Their reunion had been less stressful than she'd expected and if she would let her help instead of hanging so tightly onto her independence she, Jenna, could combine a part-time job somewhere with looking after her.

As she was clearing away after breakfast she heard a familiar voice on the terrace where her parents were sitting in the sun, and when she went outside Ethan Lomax observed her in surprise.

'Jenna!' he exclaimed. 'Have you come back to us, or is it just a visit?'

'I'm back,' she told him, smiling her pleasure at the sight of the good-natured doctor who had taken her mother's place. 'I haven't discussed it with Mum and Dad yet as I only arrived yester-day, but I would like to combine looking after her with some sort of part-time nursing somewhere.'

'I can manage….' her mother started to protest.

Ignoring the protest, Ethan was smiling and saying, 'You need look no further if you want a job. We need a part-time practice nurse to help with morning surgery, and for a couple of afternoons to assist Lucas in the cardiology clinic.'

'Lucas! Cardiology clinic!' she exclaimed. 'Who might he be? And how long has the surgery been able to offer that kind of thing?'

'Since a friend of mine needed a change of scene,' he said with a smile. 'So are you interested?'

'Of course I am!' she hooted, 'just as long as Mum and Dad agree.'

'You already know my views regarding you joining the practice,' her mother said.

Her father commented gently, 'It's all right by me, but I don't want you to feel that now you're back you're being hemmed in with our affairs, Jenna. You've got a top degree in nursing, remember.'

'Yes, I know,' she replied, 'but a nurse is a nurse is a nurse wherever he or she may be. My stepping into that role here has been delayed, but I always intended to join the practice one day if there was a place for me. We Balfour women have to stick together.'

The saying of that sentiment would have stuck in her throat at one time, she thought, but there was something so sad in seeing her mother defeated by illness that she'd meant every word.

Ethan was checking his watch. 'Must go,' he said, 'or they'll be thinking at the surgery that I've got lost. So are we sorted, Jenna? You're interested in coming to join us?'

'Yes. Definitely.'

She would have agreed to sweep the streets, or empty waste bins, if it would have resulted in the same degree of happiness she was seeing on her mother's face.

'Call in this afternoon for a chat if you get the chance,' he said as she walked to the gate with him. He lowered his voice. 'It must have been a shock when you saw your mother. She was fine when you left, wasn't she?'

'Yes, she seemed to be,' she told him sombrely. 'I had no idea, and needless to say she didn't tell me what was going on. That isn't her way.'

'I know,' he agreed, 'and it isn't always the best.'

When he'd gone her father said by way of explanation, 'Ethan calls every morning on his way to the surgery to make sure we're all right. He's a good guy.'

It was late afternoon before Jenna got the chance to call in at the practice and when she went through the main doors into Reception she was gripped by a feeling of unreality. This had been her mother's domain and now here *she* was, another Balfour about to become part of The Tides practice.

There was a new face behind Reception and as Jenna moved across to explain why she was there, the door of a consulting room opened directly behind her. As she swivelled round, there he was again, the mystery man, surfer, property owner, and what else—patient, doctor, medical sales rep?

The questions crowding her mind were soon answered as with a swift glance in her direction he said to the elderly man about to depart, 'I want to see you again next week, Mr Enderby, and if in the meantime the fast heartbeat or breathing problems return send for me immediately and we'll take it further. The ECG you've just had didn't show any cause for concern at the moment, but do remember that my heart clinic is here for your benefit.'

'It was probably me getting so worked up about losing my sheepdog that caused me to be the way I was,' the elderly farmer said awkwardly. 'I'd had Jess for a long time.'

'So maybe it wasn't surprising, then,' he said with a sympathetic smile, and Jenna thought that it must just be her that he couldn't take to. Yet why should this stranger want to get to know her? He might be living alone but there was nothing to say that he didn't prefer it that way, or wasn't already spoken for.

George Enderby halted in his tracks when he saw her standing there and exclaimed, 'Jenna! How long have you been back in Bluebell Cove, my dear?'

'Since yesterday,' she told him with a wide smile.

'And are you staying?'

'Yes, I am, Mr Enderby. I'm going to be working mornings here and will be helping with the new heart clinic on two afternoons.'

'That's good news. I feel better already.' He chortled and went slowly on his way, leaving her to adjust to the fact that the man on the beach was the Lucas person, the celebrity who was involved with the practice.

He was a new face there, just as the reception-ist seemed to be, and she, Jenna, would be another when she joined the staff. Though she wouldn't be a new face to everyone. To most folk she would be Barbara's daughter.

Only that morning Ethan had referred to a car-diologist who had his own clinic there, and this just had to be him with a dark suit and smart shirt and tie replacing the swimming trunks of their first meeting and the sports shirt and shorts that had been his attire on the second.

The elderly farmer had gone and now the receptionist was on the phone to a patient and the man observing her with cool dark eyes said, 'I'm presuming that you are Jenna Balfour here to see Ethan. He said to look after you if he wasn't back from an urgent home visit he's been called out on, but I'm sure that the receptionist will be only too pleased to make you a cup of tea when she comes off the phone.'

His tone implied that he didn't want the responsibility of looking after her and she told him frostily, 'I'll be fine, thanks just the same. It seems as if you have quite rightly decided who I am, so how about introducing yourself?'

'Lucas Devereux,' he said evenly, 'recuperating in the countryside and involving myself in medicine at a slower pace.'

She held out a smooth ringless hand and said, 'Pleased to meet you, Dr Devereux.'

He hesitated for a second then took it in a firm clasp and instead of greeting her in a similar fashion merely said, 'Nice of you to say so.'

The receptionist had replaced the phone and

he didn't waste a second in saying, 'And now, if you will excuse me, I have a patient waiting.'

'Yes, of course,' she said. 'I'll go and seek out someone that I *know* after I've introduced myself to this lady.'

CHAPTER TWO

'JENNA! So you really are back! I didn't believe Ethan when he told me he'd seen you this morning,' Lucy Watson cried when she opened the door of the nurses' room to her knock.

'Hello, Aunt Lucy,' she said, hugging the sparse frame of her mother's only friend and confidante. 'Dad phoned to ask me to come home because of how Mum is, and I came as soon as I could. I had no idea what was going on behind the scenes when I went away or I would never have gone, and now that I've seen her I'm appalled.'

'Yes, I'm sure you are,' her mother's friend said consolingly. She had been senior practice nurse for almost as long as Barbara had been in charge of the coastal medical centre. 'I told your mother countless times that she should put you in the picture, but we both know what she's like. Barbara will choke on her own pride one of these days.

'But enough of the past. Let's talk about the present. Ethan tells me that you're going to join us part time and spend the rest looking after your mother. That is really good news. Your father has been coping wonderfully but Keith needs some help, so who better than his lovely daughter who is also a nurse?

'Any problems will come from your mother's side of the arrangement. She is so used to dealing with the sick and suffering that becoming one of them herself has been hard to accept, as you can imagine. What sort of a welcome did you get?'

Jenna smiled. 'Reasonable enough. We actually had a laugh together.'

'Wow!' Lucy exclaimed. 'Seriously, though, be patient with her, Jenna. Her life has changed unbelievably.'

'I'm not short on patience,' she said soberly.

'One needs it in plenty to be a nurse. It's my mum who has always been short on it, at least where Dad and I are concerned.'

The other woman sighed. 'Yes, I agree, but knowing your father, Keith won't let you take on too much of the burden. The situation is that now Barbara needs a woman's care. The fact that you are home and will be around *and* are about to join us here at the practice is wonderful news.'

'That's what I thought,' Jenna said wryly, 'but I've just had a lukewarm reception from the cardiologist who is now part of the practice and Ethan wants me to assist him with his clinic on the two afternoons that he's here. We've already met briefly on two occasions and I get the feeling that he disapproves of me for some reason so he won't be laying down the red carpet for his new assistant.'

Lucy smiled. 'Don't be put off by his manner. Lucas Devereux is quite something in the medical world in these parts. Until recently he was top cardiologist at Hunters Hill Hospital and we couldn't believe it when he agreed to move here at Ethan's suggestion. It seems that the two of them are friends from way back.'

'Even so, why lower his sights to that extent if he was top dog at The Hill?'

'Some guy went berserk and attacked him when one of his family died during an operation that he was performing, and Lucas nearly lost his life as well.

'I've also heard tales of a broken engagement round about that time, so it's not surprising that he isn't full of the joys of spring, or should I say summer.'

Before Jenna had time to digest the distressing facts that Lucy had just passed on to her, Ethan's voice could be heard outside in the corridor. A moment later he appeared, smiling his pleasure to see her there, and she thought that here was a man who was always the same, no matter what life dealt out to him, and he'd had his own share of ups and downs in the not so recent past.

'I've just spoken to Lucas,' he told her, 'and he says that the two of you have already met.'

'Yes, we bumped into each other on the beach

yesterday, and when I went for a stroll yesterday evening he was cutting the grass outside
The Old Chart House, which he told me now
belongs to him.'

'Hmm, that is so,' he said. He turned to Lucy.
'Do you mind if I take Jenna away from you for
a little while?'

The elderly practice nurse was smiling as she
told him, 'Of course not, Dr Lomax. Knowing
that she's back and is joining the practice has
brightened my day.'

'So are you really ready to come and join us here
at The Tides?' Ethan asked when they were seated
in the office at the back of the surgery building.

'Yes,' she said firmly, 'if you're sure that you
want me on the staff, but as I said this morning
I want to help look after my mother too.'

'Of course you do,' he agreed, 'but you are going
to need some life away from the house, Jenna. You
are young and bright and will liven up this place.
The patients will love you and so will the staff.'

'Oh, yes?' she said doubtfully, with the memory
of Lucas's critical appraisal still very clear.

Ignoring the comment, he said, 'So how about mornings, eight-thirty until twelve, and Monday and Thursday afternoons assisting Lucas in the heart clinic? Do you think you could manage that with your mother to care for as well?'

This is the moment to say I can manage the mornings but not the afternoons, she was thinking. Did she want to work in such close contact with Lucas Devereux?

'I can certainly manage the mornings,' she told him. 'Mum is always up early. I can see to it that she is bathed and dressed before I leave and Dad will organise their breakfasts. Could I give the afternoons a trial before I commit myself on that?'

'Yes, of course,' he said easily. 'I haven't mentioned it to Lucas yet so a trial it shall be, say, for a couple of weeks, and then we'll have another chat.'

Unaware that he was the subject of their conversation, Lucas had just seen his last patient on their way and was thinking about his meetings with Jenna Balfour. Why couldn't he have been more pleasant, he thought, instead of giving in to an insane urge to put out her light for no other reason than someone had extinguished his own?

When he'd seen her frolicking around with the lifeguard on the beach the day before, his lip had curled at the spectacle, but who was he to criticise the light-hearted actions of others because *his* heart lay heavy as a stone?

Taking his jacket off a hanger behind the door, he picked up his case and went into the outer corridor just as Jenna, having finished her chat with Ethan, was saying goodbye to Lucy.

'Tell your mum I'll pop round for a while this evening if she feels up to it,' she was saying. 'Give me a ring if she's not, Jenna, and I'll come some other time.'

The girl with hair like sunlight was smiling, but there was something wistful in her expression as she said, 'Mum has always been happy to see you, Aunt Lucy.'

There were tears on her lashes as she gave the elderly practice nurse a parting hug and when she turned to go she found Lucas observing her once again with the unreadable dark hazel gaze that was becoming familiar.

At the main door of the surgery he was close behind and held the door for her to go through. She quickened her step to get away from him and he surprised her by saying, 'So what arrangements have you made with Ethan?'

She came to a halt and turned slowly to face him, surprised that he was aiming the question at her instead of the head of the practice, in the light of his previous manner. Suddenly her pent-up resentment of his attitude towards her came to the fore and she said, 'I'm not sure that you would want to hear it.'

Dark brows were rising as she went on, 'It is quite clear that you disapprove of me, though heaven knows why as you hardly know me. Yet I suppose it is possible to feel an immediate aversion to someone right from the moment of meeting. That being so, maybe Ethan would be the best person to explain what his plans are for me.

'I'm told that life has not been kind to you of late and I'm sorry to hear that,' she told him without pausing for breath. 'I saw the scar when we were on the beach and felt the injustice of it when I discovered from where it came. As for the inward hurts that come from broken relationships I'm sure that they too must be very painful, though I haven't had that sort of experience myself.'

'Have you quite finished?' he asked dryly.

'Er, yes,' she said hurriedly, as the verbal floodgates that had opened suddenly closed. 'And do please forgive me for being so intrusive. I don't know what came over me. Feel free to tell me to mind my own business.'

Before he could reply she began to walk quickly towards the seashore and home, and it wasn't until she reached the headland that she stopped for breath and stood cringing at the thought of how she'd behaved.

She couldn't believe that she'd let someone she hardly knew get to her to such an extent. Maybe it was because she was desperate for him to like her…and he didn't.

She hadn't looked back. If she had she would have seen a grim smile on his face as he thought that she'd managed to refrain from saying, 'Don't take your misfortunes out on me,' but it was quite clear that she'd thought it and who could blame her?

Lucy had come as promised and as she watched Jenna wandering restlessly from room to room in the warm summer night she said, 'I'll see to Barbara when she's ready for bed if you want to go out.'

'Would you, Aunt Lucy?' she said gratefully. She was desperate to speak to Lucas Devereux again before the day ended, knowing that she wouldn't be able to sleep if she hadn't apologised for her incredible outburst. If he hadn't liked her before he must detest her now, she kept telling herself, and not without good reason.

The same crowd as the night before was outside the pub as she went past but she hardly noticed them. She was praying that when she reached his house he would be there.

He was and when he answered her ring on the doorbell Lucas was wearing paint-splashed jeans, a shirt in a similar condition, and was holding a paintbrush. As he stepped back to let her in she said with the same kind of rush as when she'd said her piece the first time, 'I've come to apologise.'

'There is no need,' he said levelly. 'You are entitled to your opinion.'

She was observing him slack-jawed. Was this the sardonic stranger who had never been out of her thoughts from the first moment they'd met and was now climbing down off his pedestal?

'It is generous of you to say so,' she said gravely, 'but none of us know when life will change for the better or for the worse. When I thought about it afterwards I realised that I must have sounded extremely smug and preachy.'

'Forget it,' he insisted in the same flat tone. He pointed to a can of paint. 'What do you think of white for the paintwork in the hall? Everywhere in this place is so drab and dark colours are so depressing.'

'Er, yes, you can't go wrong with white,' she said awkwardly, with the feeling that she'd stepped on to some sort of roller-coaster that was going in the wrong direction.

It was more nerve-racking to be on good terms with Lucas Devereux than bad. Had the man any idea how attractive he was? He made all other guys she'd ever met seem pale by comparison, but if she was going to have to work with him it would be a case of keeping her mind on what she was there for, and wondering what it would feel like to be in his arms would not be on the agenda.

She'd walked up from the headland in the summer dusk and now the daylight had finally gone. The moon was dominating the heavens in a cloudless sky and conscious that she'd interrupted what he'd been doing Jenna said, 'I must go. I've left Aunt Lucy with my mum so she's all right, but I don't want to be away too long.'

He didn't comment but gave her a strange look and then took her by surprise again by saying, 'If you'll hang on while I change my clothes, I'll walk you home.'

'There's no need,' she said hastily. 'I know the way. I've done it a thousand times.'

'Nevertheless, I am not going to let you walk home alone,' he told her decisively. 'Make yourself comfortable on the sofa in the sitting room. I will be just a couple of minutes.'

He was as good as his word. She sensed that he always would be and would have scant patience with anyone who wasn't.

They'd been walking in silence for a few moments and out of the blue Lucas asked, 'So where is your lifeguard friend tonight?'

Jenna swivelled to face him, eyes widening in surprise at the question 'You mean Ronnie?'

He nodded. 'Yes, if that's his name.'

'He will be down on the beach, or with his wife and family, I would imagine, but why do you ask?' He didn't reply and as light began to dawn she exclaimed in slow surprise, 'Ah! I see!

When we were larking about yesterday you came to the conclusion that there was more to it than just a laugh between friends, which was rather presumptuous on your part, don't you think?

'Ronnie has lived here all his life, just as I have. We were in junior school at the same time, though he was on the point of leaving when I started as there is a few years' difference in our ages. He knows me best from me being on the beach. I've always used it a lot, *and* I'm godmother to one of his children.'

'All right!' he protested. 'I get the picture, and you are correct in pointing out in a roundabout way that it is none of my business.'

He wasn't going to tell her that he was piqued because she was turning out to be different from what he'd expected, that he'd *wanted* her to be the laughing blonde in a bikini flirting with the handsome lifeguard, because it fitted in better with his present jaundiced views on beautiful women.

Next he'd be discovering that Jenna Balfour

hadn't really deserted her parents when she'd been needed—the kind of criticism he'd heard from some of the village folk who thought highly of her mother's years of devoted care for the patients at The Tides.

They'd reached the headland. The lighted windows of Four Winds were shining out in the darkness and she said gravely, 'Thank you for walking me home, Lucas, but before you go, can I ask you a question?'

'Of course,' he told her smoothly, half expecting what was coming next.

'Do you always make a snap judgement on meeting someone for the first time?'

'In my work, never!' he replied, then, as Philippa drifted into his mind, he went on, 'But I was guilty of that kind of thing not so long ago and paid a high price for my gullibility with regard to a beautiful woman. I apologise for letting my first glimpse of another equally beautiful woman cause me to form what now seems to be the wrong opinion, if that is what you want me to say?'

'Only if it is really meant,' she said coolly. 'We haven't got off to a very good start, have we? If we are going to be working together we need to clear the air so that when Ethan passes on to you his suggestion that I assist you in your Monday and Thursday afternoon clinics you will have had time to decide if you are prepared to be in such close proximity to me.'

'It will depend on if you've had any experience of cardiology nursing more than anything else,' he said dryly. 'Have you?'

'Yes,' she replied. 'I've worked on a coronary unit in France, but when Ethan suggested that I assist in your clinic I asked that I might give it a trial first.'

'For what reason? You've just said that you have some experience.'

'You were the reason. I sensed your antipathy towards me.'

'And how do you feel about that now?'

She was smiling. 'Better, I think, because it seems that you might be human after all.'

The sardonic smile was back. Most nurses

he'd worked with had treated him with rever-
ence and respect. But here was a free spirit
amongst the nursing fraternity who wasn't all
that keen to work with him and there were all
the ingredients of a challenge in that.

'So I'll see you on Thursday afternoon, then?'
he questioned as they stood looking down at the
foam-tipped waves lapping onto the beach in
the moonlight.

'Er, yes, if you're going to agree to what
Ethan wants.'

'I've known him a long time. Ethan Lomax is
a good friend,' he told her sombrely. 'He saved
my sanity when he persuaded me to move to
Bluebell Cove. His plans for the practice will be
my top priority as long as I am involved in it so,
yes, I'm going to agree to you working with me.'

'Who is assisting you now?'

'No one as yet. Today's clinic was only the
second one and we were still looking for a
nurse. You appeared at just the right time,' he
told her, and hoped that she realised he was
speaking from a medical point of view. As far

as he was concerned, there would never be a right time for anything more personal.

As he walked back to his own place Lucas was thinking that from what he'd seen of her so far there appeared to be nothing devious about the beautiful Jenna Balfour, and added to that she had the personality, and hopefully the nursing experience, that he would require from her in the cardiology clinic.

For the first time in ages he was actually feeling cheerful as he climbed the stairs to the drab main bedroom of his newly acquired property, but he knew it wouldn't last. He was surrounded by too many dark shadows and broken dreams.

'Do you want to take the car?' Keith asked when Jenna came downstairs the next morning looking trim and competent in the dark blue dress of the practice nurse that Lucy had brought for her the night before.

'No. I'll walk,' she said. 'You'll need the car if you have to take Mum anywhere. The first chance I get I'll sort out some transport of my own. Which reminds me, is my bike still in the outhouse?'

He smiled. 'Yes, knowing how much you used to love the thing, I've taken great care of it while you've been away.'

She gave him a hug and her mother, seated nearby, nodded approvingly at the idea of Jenna cycling to the practice instead of walking. A feeling of rare contentment had come over her when she'd seen her daughter dressed for the surgery, and some of the pain of her own limitations had disappeared.

There'd been a lot of time to fill since she'd had to hand the practice over to Ethan, and she thought frequently that if she had to do it all over again, these two who loved her unconditionally would be first of all her priorities.

A promise she'd made way back to another loved one, long gone, had driven her through the years to a greater degree than she should have allowed it to, and now she was praying that she hadn't left it too late to be the wife and mother she should have been.

Ethan was Lucas's nearest neighbour, residing in a recently erected detached house that the builder had been inspired to grace the front of with an assortment of attractive pebbles from along the coastline.

It was only a few yards from the practice, which was a bonus as he and his wife had recently separated and the close proximity to his job made coping with the break-up a little easier. But nothing was going to take away the hurt of being apart from his children, Kirstie, eleven, and Ben, thirteen. They were living abroad with Francine, their French mother, and although he had access to them, the life of a busy G.P. didn't allow for long absences from the practice.

The two men valued each other's friendship and rarely mentioned the women who had once been in their lives and were now part of their pasts, but each was aware that the inward hurts of broken relationships were still there, and for his part Lucas was only too happy to be there for Ethan should he need him to help with practice matters.

Both at a loose end, they went to the pub that

evening and as they chatted Lucas found the opportunity to question his friend about Jenna's addition to the staff.

'She's a great girl,' Ethan enthused, 'and Barbara will be on cloud nine to know that another member of her family has joined the staff of The Tides. Jenna is going to work mornings and if you are agreeable will assist you in your clinic two afternoons a week.'

'That sounds fine,' he said immediately, omitting to mention that he'd already heard about it from the nurse in question. 'When is she due to start?'

'Tomorrow morning,' Ethan informed him, 'which will mean that instead of just having the faithful and very experienced Lucy at one end of the scale, and young trainee Maria at the other, we'll have three practice nurses, which we've needed for some time.'

'Sounds good,' Lucas commented, and wanting to satisfy his curiosity further asked, 'So why didn't Jenna come into the practice when she graduated?'

'She wanted some freedom away from her mother. There was a big fallout because she wouldn't toe the line and off she went. But she would never have gone if her mother had told her how increasingly difficult it was to keep going with the rheumatoid arthritis progressing as it was. Some of the locals who feel Barbara Balfour can do no wrong were very critical of Jenna at the time, but those who knew and liked her understood.'

'I see,' he said dryly, as another of his suppositions went by the board. Yet he'd been half expecting it ever since he'd got to know the golden girl better.

As Lucas went for his paper the next morning to the busy general store at the far side of the surgery, Jenna was cycling towards him in the early morning sun, a smiling vision in her nurse's uniform.

'Hello, there!' he said as she stopped beside him. 'I'd forgotten that you are about to join the fray. How does it feel?'

'Scary,' she told him wryly. 'I wasn't exactly the most popular person around here when I went away. It would seem that a lot of people knew that Mum wasn't coping, but no one thought to tell me, and of course Mum hid it from me, though I was so wrapped up in my own plans I wasn't entirely blameless.'

'So your father didn't say anything?'

She smiled. 'Dad less than anyone. He wanted me to get away for a while for reasons that I won't go into, but not so much that he didn't send for me when he thought it was time I knew what the situation was.'

The smile was still there and Lucas was surprised when she went on to say, 'You see, I was brought up with one and a half parents.' And before he had the chance to comment further she placed her foot back on the pedal and prepared to ride the last few yards to the practice with a parting comment of, 'I'll see you on Thursday afternoon, Lucas, if you still want me at the clinic.'

'It is Ethan's decision that you work with me,

and you might find it hard to believe...*but I don't bite.'*

She was already moving off so he didn't know if she'd heard the last bit, and he thought grimly if that *was* what she thought, he'd asked for it by being so smugly critical of someone he'd had no yardstick to measure by. There was Philippa, of course, who'd betrayed him, but to compare Jenna with her just because she was beautiful would be an insult that she didn't deserve.

The morning was going too quickly. Lucy had greeted her with open arms, and Maria, the young trainee practice nurse, who was Ronnie's eldest daughter, had flashed her a shy smile when Jenna had presented herself at the the nurses' room.

Ethan had popped in for a moment to greet her in his usual pleasant manner and she'd felt that at least there was no criticism here. They were her friends, and even Lucas had been pleasant when they'd met unexpectedly outside the busy little store.

She'd watched while Lucy had treated the first few patients and noted that they were more concerned about their health than the fact that there was a newcomer amongst the practice nurses. When Lucy needed to go to the storeroom for supplies she said, 'I'll leave you to see to the next patient, Jenna. Maria will help you out with any surgery routine that you're not sure of.' And off she went.

In line with that comment the teenager went out on to the corridor where patients waited to be seen and came back to report that Mrs Waterson was there.

Jenna groaned inwardly as she picked up the patient's records and saw that she'd come for a three-monthly B12 injection to keep anaemia at bay. Mildred Waterson had been a great admirer of her mother and rightly so as Barbara had treated her for various illnesses over the years, all of them serious, and she'd always made a good recovery due to her care. With everyone else Mildred was vinegary and critical and that side of her nature became evident the moment she saw Jenna smiling across at her as she entered the room.

'So you're back, I see,' she said. 'Waited until your mother had gone first, though, didn't you, and now they've taken you on in the surgery. Well, I'll wait for my injection until Lucy comes back from wherever she's gone, if you don't mind.'

'Of course I don't mind, Mrs Waterson,' Jenna said quietly. 'She will only be a moment. Do take a seat.'

'Fine,' she snapped. 'I will. And how *is* your mother?'

'As well as can be expected. I am working mornings mainly so that I can be with her in the afternoons.'

'Yes, I should think so,' was the acid reply.

At that moment Lucy appeared and immediately picking up on the atmosphere said smoothly, 'Isn't it lovely to have Jenna with us, Mildred?'

'Mrs Waterson would prefer you to give her the injection, Lucy,' Jenna said quickly, before any other bad vibes were put on display.

The elderly nurse said calmly, 'Yes, fine, but

in future there will be three nurses in attendance, Mildred, and it will be a matter of which one is free.'

The next patient was George Enderby, the elderly farmer who had been to Lucas's heart clinic, and to Jenna's relief there was a twinkle in his eye when he saw her standing there.

'Hello, Jenna,' he said heartily. 'I saw you the other day, didn't I, when I'd been to see that campanologist fellow?'

'You've got that a little bit wrong, Mr Enderby,' she told him. 'Dr Devereux is a cardiologist.'

'So what do those others do then, go camping?'

'No, they are the bell ringers. The people in the bell tower who turn out for Sunday church services, weddings and funerals, and now we've got that sorted out I see that you're here for a dressing on your leg, so if you'll roll up your trousers we'll have a look at it.'

The twinkle was still there in his eye as he did as she'd suggested and she said laughingly, 'You were teasing, weren't you? Wanting me to think you didn't know that Dr. Devereux is a cardiologist.'

'I might have been, yet it was worth it if it made you smile. But, then, you'd just had Mildred Waterson in here, hadn't you? And with regard to the heart man, what a treat to have somebody like him here for us folks. The only thing is that his skills could be wasted in a place like this. I wonder what made him leave Hunters Hill Hospital to come and work in Bluebell Cove?'

'I'm sure there must have been a good reason,' she replied, as a vision of the awful scar across his chest came to mind, and she started to wonder what the effects of a physical attack and the failed romance she'd heard about could have had on him.

CHAPTER THREE

WHEN Jenna left the practice at the end of the morning Lucas was in the garden once more, and after glancing quickly across to where she was mounting her cycle he didn't attempt to make any eye contact, but what he had seen in that brief glimpse was enough to tell him that she wasn't as happy as she'd been when they'd met outside the store earlier, and he wondered what could have made her look so downcast.

He wasn't to know that although the farmer's good-natured teasing had taken away some of the hurt that Mildred Waterson's acid tongue had inflicted, the pain of being judged unfairly by some was taking away the pleasure of being back in Bluebell Cove.

She supposed that Lucas could be forgiven for

his wrong assumptions after he'd seen her on the beach with Ronnie. From what she'd heard, he might have reason not to be enamoured with the behaviour of the opposite sex. But having had experience of his brusque manner, maybe *he* wasn't the easiest of people to get along with and she would have proof if that was so when she started working with him.

Mildred Waterson was a different matter and if others were judging her in the same way, it was going to be just one more example of being in the shadow of her mother for evermore.

Yet they'd been closer than they'd ever been on the first night she'd been back home, and whatever else her mother lacked it wasn't integrity. The suggestion that she had left her when she'd needed her would not have come from Barbara. In her usual autocratic way she had wanted her daughter in the practice, but hadn't been prepared to explain why and so Jenna had refused to obey her demands.

She'd seen Lucas in the garden over the way and hoped he wasn't going to come across. On the few occasions that she'd been in his company she'd found it difficult to think straight and it was a new experience for her.

There had been a few light-hearted relationships with guys she'd met while travelling abroad, and a couple of dates locally, but none of the men she'd spent time with had made her feel as weak at the knees as the lone surfer had on the beach that day. That he turned out to be one of the bigwigs from Hunters Hill Hospital was mind-blowing.

One thing was certain, *he* wasn't going to be turned on by a part-time practice nurse, and as she cycled past his house with eyes averted Jenna wished herself far away from all the worries and uncertainties that had suddenly appeared in her life.

At that moment she wasn't to know that all was not going to be gloom. When she arrived home her father met her at the door with a wide smile, and taking her in his arms planted a kiss on her smooth brow. 'Guess what?' he said with a chortle. 'The organisers of the Harvest of the

Sea have been on to say you've been chosen to be this year's central figure.

'They asked if you would be available last year, but I had to tell them you were away, and now they must have discovered that you're back. So what do you think of that?'

'Fantastic!' she breathed as the clouds in her sky disappeared.

'I hoped you'd say that,' he replied happily. 'After all, you've taken part ever since you were small, and this year you're going to be the star.'

She was laughing, blue eyes dancing at the thought. 'So what will I be? Not a mermaid squashed into a tail or anything equally uncomfortable, I hope.'

'I don't know. You'll find out when you get in touch.'

'What does Mum think about the idea?'

'Why don't you ask her?'

She did, and Barbara said in her usual way, 'Just as long as it doesn't keep you away from the surgery, it's a very nice thought, and with regard to the practice, have you seen much of Lucas Devereux so far?'

'I've spoken to him a couple of times and will be assisting in his clinic twice weekly, so I'll have a better idea of what he's like then.'

'I believe that Lucy has told you of the recent happenings in his life?' her mother questioned.

'Er, yes, she has, though only briefly,' she said soberly. 'How awful to be attacked in the course of treating the sick.'

'Yes, indeed,' her mother agreed with a mirthless smile. 'Stress can change people with a short fuse into monsters. But as well as that he discovered that his fiancée, who was also second in command, was after his position as top surgeon on the unit and was prepared to stop at nothing to get it.'

'Ah, I see,' Jenna said slowly, 'and as he is no longer at Hunters Hill, did she get it?'

'No, the primary care trust saw to that. They've appointed a temporary replacement in the hope that Lucas will soon feel ready to take up the reins again.'

'And do you think he will?'

'Hopefully, yes. It's great to have him with us but his knowledge could be put to much better use in a big hospital.'

'And what happened to the treacherous fiancée?' Jenna questioned casually.

'She went abroad, seeking pastures new. We have to remember that there is a hierarchical attitude amongst some of the top medical people.'

'Does that include Lucas Devereux?'

'I wouldn't think so, considering what the man is doing now. His name was a byword at Hunters Hill, but he has calmly stepped down the ladder without any lessening of his dedication to cardiac patients.'

Barbara picked up a book that she'd been engrossed in at that point and Jenna went up to her room to get changed with a lot to think about, and what had happened to the man who was far too much in her thoughts came top of the list.

The rest of the day passed just as quickly as the morning had done, and the sun was setting over a calm blue sea the first time that Jenna had a moment to herself.

She'd gone outside on to the headland for a breath of air and when she looked down, Lucas was climbing up towards her from the beach, minus the surfboard on this occasion as the tide was out. He was dressed in just shorts and trainers, with the scar across his chest plain to see, and Jenna felt tears prick at the thought of the hurts he'd received because of his job.

Yet there was nothing to denote any kind of self-pity when he drew level. In the light of the dying sun he asked in the abrupt manner that she was becoming familiar with, 'What was wrong when you left the surgery this morning? You didn't look very happy.'

His presence beside her made Mildred Waterson's acrimony seem a million miles away and she answered easily, 'It wasn't anything much. A patient had just been commenting about the way I left my mother when she was ill. The fact that I had no idea how serious it was didn't come into the discussion as far as Mrs Waterson was concerned, but life isn't all doom and gloom, is it, Lucas?'

He was raising a dubious eyebrow. He had some reservations about the truth of that. 'What has happened to make you say that?' he asked.

'The Harvest of the Sea Committee has asked me to lead the yearly festival that we in Bluebell Cove hold in the fish sheds at the harbour during the first week of September. The vicar is in charge of the service and almost everyone turns out for it. I only found out today that I've been chosen and am thrilled to have been asked.'

He was actually smiling without any effort. 'So the harvest is of fish instead of produce from the fields and orchards? You'd better let me have the date. What do they do with the fish afterwards?'

'Deliver it to the old, sick and needy. What is left is cooked and we have a fish and chip supper.'

'Hmm, sounds great. What do you wear for this special occasion?'

'It varies from year to year. I'll be hearing soon as it's already the middle of August.'

'I'm amazed how different life is here compared with the town. It's like another world,' he said, 'and it's great to be here for Ethan if he needs me. The poor guy is really missing Francine and the children.'

'I've noticed that they aren't around and as I get the impression that it isn't a topic for discussion I haven't asked him why.'

'Francine has taken Kirstie and Ben to live in her parents' old home in northern France. She inherited what I'm told is a very attractive house in a beautiful village and wanted the children to have the benefit of growing up there, as she did.'

'But what about Ethan?' she gasped. 'He hasn't been senior partner in the practice for long. He wouldn't want to pack up and wave goodbye to Bluebell Cove just like that.'

'Exactly,' he agreed dryly. 'From what I've been told, the only reason your mother agreed to retire was because Ethan was going to follow in her footsteps. He was the only one she would trust her beloved practice to, and knowing him he won't let her down. But he is not the happy guy he might appear. He adores his children and now doesn't see enough of them.'

'And does he still adore Francine?'

He shrugged broad shoulders tanned by the summer sun. 'I don't know. Maybe not.' And as he turned to go he said sombrely, 'Don't let the hurts that others do to you quench your spirit, Jenna.'

Then he was gone, striding towards the house he had bought on an impulse and had since wondered if he was going to regret it, and Jenna was left with a strong desire to run after him and hold him close.

It was almost two o'clock on Thursday after-noon and Jenna had just arrived at the surgery with only seconds to spare.

'I'm sorry,' she gasped, red faced from a mixture of exertion and mortification. 'I had a puncture on the way here.'

'I see,' Lucas said coolly, his pleasure at seeing her again concealed by his tone. 'Perhaps a more reliable form of transport is needed.'

'Such as?' she questioned. 'I haven't yet had time to look for a car and when I do it will have to be something very basic until my bank balance improves.'

'There's one on my drive you can borrow.'

'What? Not the bright red sports car, surely? You wouldn't trust me with that…would you?' she exclaimed.

'Yes. Why not? I don't use it. I bought it for someone else and they're not around any more, so feel free. And now are we going to get on with what we came to do? There are patients waiting who have much more important problems than a punctured bicycle tyre.'

'Yes,' she said meekly, and he turned away to hide a smile.

'So call in the first patient, then, and show me how good you are.'

As the afternoon progressed Lucas was impressed with Jenna's knowledge and patience with those who were afraid, in pain and bewildered by what was happening to them.

Like the thirty-year-old fisherman who'd

never had a day's illness in his life and was suddenly discovering that his heart wasn't working properly and he might need surgery.

'I have to work,' he'd said raggedly. 'What I catch in the nets is what pays the bills and feeds my family.'

'So we're going to sort you out,' Lucas told him with the assumed calm that he'd displayed since he was attacked. 'I'm going to pass you over to Hunters Hill Coronary Unit for tests and will urge upon them that there should be no delay in getting you sorted. If surgery is needed I will do it, so go home and wait until they phone you. It won't be long and we'll take it from there.'

He was on the phone to the hospital the moment the fisherman had gone and Jenna wondered chokingly how anyone could have hurt him as badly as the two people who could have blighted his life if he'd been a lesser mortal.

She wondered sometimes if they had when he was in one of his brooding, non-communicative moods, though he seemed relaxed enough today. As for him offering her the use of the car, it was heart-warming and mind-blowing rolled into one, considering that most of the time she felt that she was merely being tolerated.

As far as she was concerned, if for some reason he should disappear out of her life as swiftly as he'd entered it, she would be devastated.

When the clinic was over and she was tidying away she caught Lucas staring into space, and risking a rebuke said, 'What's wrong?'

'Er, nothing.'

'But you look miserable,' she protested.

'I was thinking about how confident I sounded with the man who has just left. I will operate on you myself, I said, but supposing he has a friend or relative waiting to carve me up if something goes wrong?'

She was observing him, aghast at his train of thought. 'That would never happen twice in a lifetime,' she said gently. 'It shouldn't have happened once, yet sadly it did, but please don't let the memory of it take the purpose out of your work, Lucas. If you do that it will be a double blow. You were left with a scarred body. Don't end up with a scarred mind too.'

'I guess you're right,' he said flatly. 'I'll bear in mind what you've said the next time I see some guy reach inside his jacket.'

'And come out with his wallet or a handkerchief?'

'You're not going to give up on me, are you?' he said quizzically. 'Getting back to the car on my drive, it's insured for any driver, so if you want to go home in it and leave your bike here, I'll ride it down to your place this evening, and then perhaps we could go for a drink while you tell me how you come to know so much about coronary care.'

'Yes, all right,' she agreed, concealing her amazement.

When she arrived home in the red sports car her father came out onto the drive and observed it in amazement. 'So where has this come from?' he wanted to know.

'It's on loan,' she told him breezily.

'On loan?'

'Yes. I had a puncture on the way to the surgery and was on the last minute for the heart clinic, which didn't please Lucas Devereux. So as this was standing on his drive doing nothing, he suggested I use it for as long as I want.'

'And what have you done with the bicycle?'

'He's bringing it round this evening.'

She didn't mention what Lucas had suggested they do afterwards, as although her father would approve, her mother's approval of anything was never to be taken for granted.

Barbara had been forced into retirement before Lucas had become involved with the practice, and it went without saying that she would have made it her business to get to know him at the first opportunity that had presented itself. She would almost certainly have approved of his manner, appearance and most of all his reputation at Hunters Hill, so him turning up on her daughter's bicycle might be something of a let-down.

As she was changing into one of her most

attractive dresses that evening, Jenna glanced through her bedroom window and saw Lucas, dressed in shorts and an open-necked shirt, cycling down the slope from the village on the old bike in question, and wondered what her mother would think of him now.

She considered whether she should invite him in for a drink, and at the same time introduce him to her father, whose interest in the red sports car was not dwindling.

But did she want Lucas to feel that she was making too much of his offer to return the bike and take her for a drink afterwards? Cringing at the idea, she flicked a brush through her hair and hurried down to greet him as he swerved onto the drive.

She was spared having to decide whether to introduce him to her parents as at that moment her father came strolling casually from round the back of the house and as she introduced them it became inevitable that her mother must not be denied the pleasure of a chat, so she invited Lucas inside to lighten up her day a little.

While he was bringing a rapidly brightening Barbara up to date with what was going on at the practice, Keith went into the kitchen to make coffee, and Jenna went upstairs to finish getting ready, unaware that Lucas was tuned in to her discomfiture at having to parade him in front of her parents, and even more unaware of how much he wished that he was part of a close family.

During his ill-fated relationship with Philippa he'd had visions of her presenting him with the children he longed for, but had discovered to his cost that her *cravings* were very different to his.

When Jenna came downstairs and glanced at him warily, he flashed her a reassuring smile and saw some of the tension leave her expression. When they were outside he said, 'You're fortunate to have a family who care for you, and that you care about in return.'

She was smiling now that the ordeal was over. 'I love my dad totally,' she told him, 'but he and I have always come second in my mother's life.'

'I take it that you're referring to the practice?'

'Yes. She has always been ready to go the

extra mile for her patients and is revered and re-spected by them all. I understood Mildred Waterson's comments the other day even though they were hurtful, but apart from Lucy, who is a dear, not many people know anything about our home lives. In fact, you are the only person I've ever discussed it with—which is strange, you being a dedicated doctor yourself.'

Not so dedicated that he would neglect his family if he had one, Lucas thought. His expression was sombre. How could anyone not put a child first, especially one that was their own flesh and blood? But it happened, and from what he'd learnt about his ex-fiancée when they had been splitting up, prestige would have come first with Philippa.

But it was a glorious summer night, the duplicity of one woman and an over-zealous approach to her career of another should not be allowed to put clouds in the sky and he said, 'How about a stroll along the beach before we have that drink?'

'Yes,' Jenna said immediately, and he thought

how uncomplicated and lacking in guile she was. He could visualise her golden fairness accentuated by some sort of mermaid outfit at the Harvest of the Sea, and knew it was something he was not going to miss, even though he kept telling himself that no way was he going to get too close to her.

His judgement had been wrong once and he wasn't going to make a habit of it. He'd mistaken Philippa's sense of purpose for integrity and it had been anything but. If he let himself become entranced by the girl walking barefoot beside him on the sand he would need his head examined.

Yet he'd opened up to her that afternoon as he hadn't done to anyone else, even Ethan, and that had to mean something.

The shoes she'd taken off were dangling from her hand by their straps and looking down to the fingers grasping them the memory surfaced of the large solitaire diamond that had graced the hand of his ex-fiancée and he asked, 'Does no rings mean no relationships?'

He'd asked the question in a detached sort of way but it brought Jenna to a halt, and when she turned to face him it was as if their roles were reversed, that she was the older and wiser of the two of them as she said coolly, 'A ring on one's finger means nothing if the right kind of love isn't there, but since you ask, no, I'm not attracted to *anyone* at the present time.'

It was far from the truth, but the man beside her could be on the rebound from what must have been a disastrous relationship and there was no way that she wanted him to get the idea that she would be available if he should beckon.

The sand beneath her feet was moist and as she began to move forward at a faster pace the imprint of them was there to indicate that she'd passed that way, but not for long. It would disappear with the next incoming tide and there was nothing to say that Lucas Devereux's entrance into her life wouldn't be the same, leaving her in a lovelorn state of limbo.

He was groaning inwardly. The set of her shoulders told him he hadn't handled *that* very well. He must be insane to have upset this beautiful, uncomplicated woman by a thoughtless chance remark.

Yet the fact remained he had wanted to know if he was butting into another man's territory by spending time with her. She'd made it clear he wasn't doing *that*, but he'd put his foot in it by asking.

'So are we still going for a drink?' he asked when he caught up with her.

'If you insist,' was the reply.

'I'm not insisting. I'm just asking,' he said abruptly, and Jenna felt that maybe she was making a big thing out of a little one.

'Yes, why not?' she agreed. 'But unless you want us both to be recognised by half of Bluebell Cove maybe we should try somewhere further along the coast, or drive into the country.'

'Why? Don't you want to be seen with me?'

'It's *your* reputation I'm thinking of,' she said laughingly, her good humour returning. 'Your arrival in this place has caused quite a stir, and for you to be seen with the black sheep of the community won't do it any good.'

'I think you might be exaggerating some-what,' he told her, dark eyes glinting with amusement. 'The only people in Bluebell Cove who are getting a buzz from me being there are those with heart problems.

'To the rest I'm just another doctor at the practice, and if we're going to drive out into the country we need to go as the sun is setting and there isn't a moon as yet. Owls will soon be hooting and all the little creatures of the night will come scuttling out of their hidey holes.

'The Red Peril is parked on your parents' drive so we might as well use it. I'm sure there must be some nice places not too far away where we can relax for an hour or so. If it had been earlier in the day we could have had a cream tea.'

'That is what Mum and Dad were having somewhere out in the countryside when I arrived back home that first day. It was rather an anticlimax as I'd been expecting her to be virtually housebound, but when they arrived home and I saw her get out of the car, I knew the score.

'Dad had phoned to say where they were and that it could be a couple of hours before they got back, so if you remember I decided to go down to the beach which was surprisingly empty except for Ronnie the lifeguard…*and you casting a dubious glance in my direction.*'

She was waiting for him to say something, but he just pursed his lips into an enigmatic smile and let the comment pass. Seconds later a lazy moon was coming into view from behind a cloud and they were driving between hedges laden with summer flowers, and behind them in sweeping green fields was the gorse.

It could have been a magical occasion, the two of them close in the low-slung car beneath a summer moon, Jenna thought, but they were both wary of each other, hadn't known each other long enough to be comfortable in the situation they found themselves in.

Down on the beach it had been all right. Strolling along the sand without any particular closeness hadn't created any chemistry that they couldn't cope with. But now it was different, with her wanting the friendly camaraderie that was establishing itself to continue without any undercurrents, and Lucas vowing that if he drove himself crazy in the attempt he wasn't going to give her cause for thinking he was on the rebound.

All of which contributed to a rather stilted atmosphere when they stopped at a country pub with a thatched roof and horse brasses gleaming everywhere. 'You're thinking this is a mistake, aren't you?' he said as they took their drinks into a pleasant beer garden at the side of the building. 'That we have little in common to discuss but medicine.'

She shrugged her smooth golden shoulders, but didn't reply because there were a thousand things she would like to talk to him about, instead of what they did for a living.

It was only days since she'd first seen him on the beach and every time she thought about it she felt as if she'd been waiting all her life for him to appear. Yet every time she'd been near him since, the pleasure had always been tempered with the feeling that maybe Lucas was seeking some kind of temporary solace and was singling her out to fill the gap. She still sensed bitterness in him.

They drank in silence and the moment their glasses were empty he asked if she would like a refill. When she shook her head he got to his feet and held out his hand for her to do likewise.

It was the first time they'd touched and if the atmosphere had been less grim Jenna would have thought of it as a moment to cherish rather than an act of brief courtesy on his part.

They drove back to the headland and when he stopped the car on the drive of her parents' house Lucas said, 'I'll see you at Monday's clinic if not before. Ethan has some stressful days ahead and I want to give him all the help I can, so we might meet at the surgery before then. He tells me he and Francine are getting divorced, which is an absolute catastrophe. They were always so happy, I just can't believe it.'

Forgetting her forebodings and uncertainties, she reached across, kissed him swiftly on the cheek, and told him as he observed her in surprise, 'You are clearly a good friend to him, and it seems to me that anyone who has you for a friend is blessed.'

Already regretting her impulsiveness, she was moving swiftly towards the front door of the house, leaving him to switch off the engine and ease himself slowly out of the car.

As it closed behind her he began to walk slowly up the slope to the village.

Ethan was sitting outside on his patio, having a last drink of the day, and he shouted across for Lucas to join him.

'What has happened to the sports car?' was the first thing he said when they were seated side by side.

'I've lent it to my assistant. Jenna had a puncture on her way to the clinic this afternoon and was on the last minute. As her bike is the only transport she's got at the moment I told her she could use the car for as long as she needs to.'

'How did she do with the heart patients?' Ethan asked.

'Great. She's pleasant, has lots of patience, and is very knowledgeable considering it isn't long since she graduated.'

'Her mother would be pleased to know that. It has always been her wish that Jenna should join the practice, but Barbara doesn't always go about those kinds of things in the right way.'

'*Did* she leave her mother in the state she's in now and go off to do her own thing?' Lucas questioned once again.

'No, I told you. Some of the old die-hards like to feel she did, but Barbara was concealing her worsening condition to a great extent—she has a dread of being an object of pity. So, determined to throw off her bonds once and for all, Jenna packed her bags and went, but you can rest assured that she wouldn't have done if her mother had come clean about her worsening health.'

There was surprise in his expression as he went on to say, 'I wouldn't have expected *you* to be in touch with the comings and goings of the locals. Do I take it that someone has been getting at Jenna?'

Lucas nodded. 'Yes, someone called Mildred Waterson gave her a hard time.'

'Surprise! Surprise! Mildred Waterson would have Barbara canonised if it was possible, but why all the interest in Jenna? Do I detect the healing of a broken heart?'

'It wasn't broken,' he protested. 'I consider myself to have had a lucky escape, and any further ventures into romance will be a long time coming.'

CHAPTER FOUR

LUCAS was nowhere around on the Friday after their drive into the countryside the previous night, and when Ethan explained that he was in the process of transferring his belongings from a luxury apartment near the hospital to The Old Chart House, Jenna understood his absence.

Ethan had called the staff together before surgery started and told them that he too would be unavailable during the coming week as he was flying to France on Monday to see his children.

'Lucas will take charge while I'm gone,' he told them, 'and we have a new doctor starting first thing Monday morning to help ease the workload. His name is Leo Fenchurch and he's really keen to gain some experience in general practice, having previously been hospital based.'

'Is he to replace Francine?' Lucy asked, and Jenna saw Ethan's jaw tighten.

'Possibly,' he replied.

With that the morning had got under way and with the nurses' room as busy as always Jenna didn't have time to dwell on the comings and goings of staff at the practice, except to be relieved that Lucas was still going to be with them.

Francine had been a G.P. there alongside her husband before she'd inherited the house in France, but when the overwhelming urge to go and live there had overtaken her she'd gone against her husband's wishes and taken the children with her, leaving a vacancy at the surgery that needed to be filled.

The split had occurred while Jenna had been abroad and she'd known nothing about it until her first day there as a part-time nurse. She'd been appalled to hear that a marriage that she would have expected to last for ever had foundered.

Francine had always been a loving mother and wife and had seemed settled in the UK where both their jobs were, so it was totally out of character for her to have created the present situation.

Jenna's first patient of the day was Meredith Slater, who owned a guest house on the road that led to the beach. She was a pleasant, capable woman in her fifties, and her good cooking and spotless accommodation kept a steady flow of satisfied visitors returning regularly to Bluebell Cove.

Today she was subdued and pale and the notes that Ethan had brought to the nurses' room after he'd examined her indicated that he wanted blood tests done for a manner of things, including thyroid, diabetes, calcium levels and anaemia.

'We don't often see you here, Meredith!' Lucy exclaimed as Jenna was following his instructions.

'I know,' she agreed. 'I've just told Dr Lomax that I feel like an engine that is running out of power. I'm tired all the time, totally listless, and that's no good in a business like mine. I can hardly get out of bed in the mornings as I ache all over.'

Jenna nodded. 'He has asked for an ESR test as well, Meredith.'

'What is that for?'

'When a woman over fifty complains of not being able to get out of bed she can be suffering from polymyalgia and an ESR test is done to check the amount of inflammation present.'

'Inflammation where?'

'In the muscles rather than the joints, and as soon as it has been diagnosed the patient is prescribed steroids, usually a drug called prednisolone, and the symptoms disappear almost immediately.'

'It's as simple as that?'

'Not exactly. It can take a couple of years for the sufferer to come off the steroids as it has to be a very gradual process, but polymyalgia usually clears up eventually. So let's wait and see what the tests show up and in the meantime can you get some help in the guest house?'

'Yes. My husband has taken early retirement

and we're going to run it together from now on, but I'll feel happier when I know what is wrong with me.'

At the other end of the passage Ethan was closeted with an elderly man who had been rushed into hospital in the middle of the night with a serious nosebleed that had not stopped until it had been cauterised by an ear, nose and throat specialist, and having been told by someone that it could be a sign of a serious form of leukaemia he was there seeking reassurance.

'I've had a report from the hospital and there was nothing in the blood tests that they took to indicate anything of that sort,' he told him reassuringly.

'It was more a case of the membranes inside your nose becoming drier and thinner because of your age and the hot temperatures of summer. Also the fact that you are on a reduced dosage of aspirin to keep your heart healthy and prevent strokes will have made your blood thinner. That is why the force of the bleed was so unsus-

tainable until the inside of your nose was cauterised. However, having said all that, I will ask
for another blood test just to be on the safe side.

'If you will go and wait outside the nurses'
room, one of them will do that for you and we
should have the results back within a week. Did
the doctor from Ear, Nose and Throat tell you to
put Vaseline inside your nose?'

'Aye, and they said not to blow it, or try to
hold it back when I want to sneeze,' was the
reply, 'but I've never had any patience with
people who spread their germs around by
sneezing all over the place.' And off he ambled
in the direction of the nurses' room.

When Jenna arrived home in the car that Lucas
had lent her without a moment's hesitation, she
noticed a magazine pushed towards the back of
the glove compartment, and when she reached
across for it saw that it was the winter edition
of Hunters Hill Hospital's report on patient care,
new ventures, finance and various other items
of interest to those employed there.

After glancing through it briefly, she was about to put it back when she noticed that the back cover was given over to photographs of the staff ball on the previous New Year's Eve and clearly on view amongst those present was Lucas with a tall, strikingly attractive, flame-haired woman by his side, and if she'd had any doubts about her identity the caption beneath would have banished them as it said, *Lucas Devereux, the Hospital's Leading Cardiovascular Surgeon, with his Fiancée and Second in Command, Philippa Carswell.*

Jenna sighed as she put the magazine back where it belonged. The engagement may have foundered, but that was clearly the kind of woman that Lucas was attracted to and she was nothing like her.

Small, petite almost, with fair colouring that would look insipid against the dark allure of the woman in the picture, it was amazing that he had even noticed her, let alone wanted to spend time with her, and the feeling that Lucas might be looking for a stopgap was stronger than ever.

It was fortunate that she wouldn't be seeing him over the weekend. It would give her time to cool down, and as part of the process she was going to find a car that suited her budget and return the sports car to its owner.

She'd promised to take her mother and Lucy clothes shopping in the town the following morning. They were going to put a fold-away wheelchair in the boot of the family car and once the two women had exhausted their interest in fashion she was going to take them to her mother's favourite restaurant for lunch.

They had to pass the hospital on their way to the shops and as she glanced casually across to the main entrance she almost lost control of the car.

The couple on the back page of the magazine were standing at the top of the steps that led to the main reception area and she thought chokingly *some* broken engagement if the body language of the woman beside him was anything to go by.

Her mother and Lucy were chatting on the

back seat and didn't see them, or notice when she increased speed, but for her the day had taken a downward plunge as it began to sink in that maybe Lucas wasn't on the rebound after all.

They arrived home in the early afternoon and when she'd settled her mother in a chair on the patio with a foot rest, a cool drink and a canopy above to keep the heat of the sun off her, Jenna went down to the beach to unwind.

The surf was tempting as the waves came crashing onto the sand and she wished she'd brought her board with her. There was a yearning within her to ride high on it, to let the dismay at her foolishness in secretly falling for a man like Lucas be wiped away by the power of the elements.

Why couldn't she have fallen in with someone with an uncomplicated life? Obviously the two of them were still in touch, though why they should have been about to go into the hospital of all places when the flame-haired woman was now based in America and Lucas was in the middle of moving house, she didn't know.

One thing was certain. He wasn't going to be striding along the beach towards her today, making her blood warm and her heart beat faster. He had other fish to fry, and, with 'fish' in mind, there was another thing.

There'd been a message waiting for her when they'd got back from the shopping trip to say that for her part in the Harvest of the Sea thanksgiving service she would be required to wear a straw boater, a blue and white striped apron, and would be carrying the largest fish of the day's catch on a silver tray, and if that 'attractive' ensemble didn't finally quench any yearnings towards her that Lucas might have had, she didn't know what would. Gone were the dreams of being a beautiful sea creature. Maybe she could rustle up a pair of clogs to finish off the outfit.

He had a busy weekend ahead of him and with the memory of the flat atmosphere between Jenna and himself on Thursday night Lucas was not feeling on top of the world when Philippa of all people had appeared on his horizon once again—at the hospital of all places.

He'd gone to collect some personal belongings that he'd left there in his locker and couldn't believe what he was seeing when they'd met in the car park.

'I'm over for my niece's wedding,' she'd said, 'and thought I'd look up some of the people from Hunters Hill while I'm here, yourself included.'

'I'm only here briefly myself,' he'd told her. 'I have a busy weekend in front of me. I've just called to pick up some of the things I left behind.'

'So you haven't come back yet?' she'd commented. 'Seems a waste.'

'A lot of things have seemed like that of late, but I'm getting sorted and am happier than I've been in a long time,' he informed her.

'So you wouldn't like to come out for a meal one evening?'

His glance was cold. 'No, thanks. I would have thought you knew better than to suggest something like that. The days are gone when we had something to say to each other. So if you'll excuse me...' And he'd gone straight to the room that had once been his and collected his belongings.

And now in the middle of the afternoon he was waiting for the van to arrive with the furniture from the apartment, and once it had been delivered he was going to see if he could find Jenna without actually knocking on the door of her house.

He was aware that he'd been abrupt with the woman he'd once intended to marry. She probably thought he hadn't forgiven her. If she did she was wrong and maybe he should have put her right about that.

Philippa had done him a favour. If they hadn't split up he would never have met Jenna who, with her clear and uncomplicated mind, seemed to understand him better than he understood himself.

She'd behaved naturally towards him almost from the moment of their meeting until the other night, and then for some reason she'd become aloof and he wasn't sure why, so he wouldn't rest until he'd seen her if only for a moment.

He could see her down on the beach when he reached the end of the coast road and his heart-beat quickened, but not for long. She was running towards where a young family had been climbing over the rocks that led upwards to the headland.

There had been excited cries from the children as they'd moved from one sea-worn rock to another but not any more. When he looked down at them he saw that the youngest child, a small girl, had slipped and was lying flat on her back on the rough, uneven surface of the rock with one of her legs twisted awkwardly beneath her.

He groaned. At one time he would have rushed to them without a moment's thought, but not now. As he clambered downwards he was bracing himself for what lay ahead, wishing that the little girl hadn't fallen, wishing that he didn't have to be a doctor again.

Until he drew level with Jenna after her upward

climb and saw the look in her eyes. It was telling him she understood what was in his mind and that it would be all right…

At that moment the child's father, horrified at the mishap that had befallen his daughter, bent to try and lift her up, and back in his doctor role he called out, 'Don't move her!

'There could be spinal injuries or broken bones,' he explained as he bent over the sobbing child. 'We need to wait until paramedics arrive. They're used to dealing with accident cases without causing further damage to fractures and suchlike.'

He glanced across at Jenna who was already on her phone, ringing A and E at Hunters Hill and explaining that a helicopter might be needed to lift the child off the rocks in the safest possible way. 'I'm going to phone the coastguard,' she told the voice at the other end of the line, 'and ask for their co-operation in winching the little girl off the rocks, as she appears to have injuries that could be serious to her back and leg. We need help fast.'

'You're not threatened by the tide, are you?' she was asked.

'No, we are halfway up the side of the cliff.'

'So hang on in there,' was the reply. 'We'll get to you as fast as we can.'

When she'd finished the call Jenna crouched beside Lucas, who was checking the little girl's pulse and heartbeat with the parents hovering anxiously nearby.

'Don't cry, sweetie,' her mother said gently. 'Some doctors and nurses are coming to look after you.'

They are here already, Lucas thought wryly as his glance met that of his fair assistant, but no point in going into that scenario. All that mattered was to get the now shivering child into the proper kind of care because as well as being injured she was in shock.

He checked her pulse again and took off the lightweight jacket he was wearing to provide extra warmth, indicating for the others to do likewise, and at the same time they heard the whirring blades of a helicopter.

It appeared within seconds and hovered above them, looking for a place to land, but there was nowhere flat or large enough and the pilot called down, 'We're going to winch paramedics down and if they decide she shouldn't be moved in the normal way they'll send the child up fastened to a backboard with a winchman in attendance to avoid jarring any injured parts. Who's in charge amongst you?'

'We are!' Lucas shouted above the noise of the engine, and pointed to Jenna. 'We are doctor and nurse.'

The pilot nodded. 'They thought from the phone message that someone who knew what they were doing was making the call.' He glanced over his shoulder, 'Hey ho! Here they come!' And two paramedics came down the winch line to land beside them.

They agreed immediately with his decision that the child should be handled as little as possible and when she'd been strapped on to a backboard, still sobbing with pain and fear, one of them took her upwards with him to the warmth and safety of the helicopter.

The family followed and Jenna and Lucas

watched them fly off into the distance in dis-
believing silence. A family stroll had turned
into a serious situation and by some miracle
the two of them had been there when they
were needed.

It had not been a good day, Lucas was
thinking. There'd been the unexpected
meeting with Philippa, which he could have
done without, and all the time simply had a
niggling longing to be with the woman
walking beside him along the headland. Only
to have their moment of meeting turned into
an emergency by a child being hurt and fright-
ened, and a family traumatised by what had
befallen them.

Maybe in the morning they would have news
of the young one's condition. He'd been crazy
to let his nightmares get to him when he'd been
clambering down the cliff side, but Jenna had
been there for him again, she'd understood.

Jenna's thoughts were running along different
lines and amongst them was surprise, the
surprise of seeing Lucas there when she'd

expected him to be with the flame-haired woman.

'Would you like to come in for a coffee?' she asked with stiff politeness when they reached her home, and he swung round to face her, taken aback by her tone.

'Er, no, thanks,' he replied. 'I've had a vanload of furniture delivered and the place is in chaos. What have you been up to?'

'I took Mum and Lucy into town to do some shopping. Then we had lunch, and now she's resting on the patio, Dad is pottering in the garden and very soon I will be making the evening meal.'

'So you haven't time to give an opinion on my decorating before I arrange the furniture?' He hoped it didn't sound as if he was begging but now that they were together he didn't want to leave her.

She looked surprised for a moment, then putting what she'd seen on the hospital steps to the back of her mind said, 'I'd love to see it and to watch you decide what is going where. I'm pushed for time now, but could come up this evening if you haven't got company.'

There'd been something meaningful about the way she'd said that and he gave a dry laugh. 'Such as who? Ethan is my only visitor and he has such a lot on his mind at present I rarely see him, but I like to be there if he's low in spirit or stressed by what is going on in his life. It must be agony being apart from his children.'

'Yes, indeed,' she agreed. 'When I have babies I won't let them out of my sight for a moment.'

A vision of her holding a golden-haired child in her arms came to mind and he could feel himself weakening in his resolve to control the attraction she had for him.

They were at the gates of the old weathered house that had been her home for as long as she could remember and she said, 'I can't come until I've got Mum settled for the night, which could be rather late. Is that all right?'

'Yes, of course,' he told her easily.

She could come in the middle of the night if she so wanted just as long as she came. She was so full of life, so easy to have around, for a little while he would feel like the man he used to be, upbeat and in control of every aspect of his life…

She arrived at nine o'clock, on foot, and when he opened the door to her Lucas exclaimed, 'Jenna, why didn't you use the car, for goodness' sake?'

'I didn't want to exploit your kindness in loaning it to me,' she explained primly. 'I'm going to get one of my own as soon as I have a moment to spare.'

He was frowning. 'Didn't I tell you I was in no hurry to have it back?'

'Yes,' she agreed, 'but nevertheless…'

He sighed. 'So what have I done to make you back away from me?'

'Nothing,' was the reply, and it was true. She was the one in the wrong for being piqued at seeing him with the woman he'd once been going to make his wife. Having seen them together only hours ago, she was dreading hearing that the engagement was back on.

She was looking around her. Lucas had transformed the drab house into a place of light and colour, and the furniture, yet to be positioned, was stylish yet old enough to fit in with the age of the property. The Old Chart House was coming into its own. All it needed now was people, living and loving there.

Lucas was watching her as they went from room to room and when they came to the master bedroom he saw her colour rise, but she was composed enough as she looked around her.

'You've made this old house beautiful,' she told him. 'Do I remember you saying when we first met that you're going to turn part of it into private consulting rooms?'

He nodded. 'Yes. There is a separate entrance where the morning room is, and on the same side of the house there is a study and a garden room that I'm going to have converted.'

'So you're not going back to heart surgery at the hospital?'

'No. Not just yet. I might do eventually, but for

the moment I need some healing time—both mind and body.'

He could have told her that she was playing a large part in that, but the healing process wasn't so far advanced that he was going to start making commitments that he might feel he couldn't keep, and there was still a slight chill in the atmosphere that told him not to push it.

'I've got some champagne on ice to celebrate. Would you care to join me?' he asked, hoping to lighten the atmosphere.

She'd gone pale. 'Celebrate what exactly?'

'Me having turned a drab mausoleum into a home. What else?'

What else indeed? Had she really seen him with that woman? she wondered.

There were flowers on a small table nearby and the card with them said, *From Philippa with love*, so what *was* she supposed to think?

Lucas was observing her thoughtfully and he said slowly, 'Did you drive past the hospital on your way to the shops this morning?'

'No. Why?'

If she'd said yes he might have put her mind at rest one way or the other, but could she cope with it?

While they were seated on tea chests, drinking the champagne, Lucas asked, 'What do you do with yourself on Sundays?'

She was on safe ground with that question and smiled across at him.

'I used to spend the day on the beach, or go sailing with my friends, but now it isn't so easy. I came home to look after my mother and that is my main concern. I always thought she was invincible but am discovering that she's human like the rest of us. Considering what she used to be like, she's coping reasonably well with what is happening to her.'

'So you are going to be on the home front all day?'

'Not all day. In the afternoon Dad always takes Mum for a cream tea, which she loves, and then they linger in the countryside for a while as it's so beautiful around here, isn't it?'

'Mmm,' he murmured, with a faster-beating

pulse as his glance took in the slender stem of her neck rising smooth and sun-kissed above the cleft of her breasts. *He'd* been hurt in mind and body, he thought, but Jenna was beautiful and untouched, which was how it should be.

She was observing him with questioning eyes above the sparkling liquid in the glass, and twirling the stem of it between her fingers she commented, 'You're miles away.'

He shook his head. She was wrong. He was exactly where he wanted to be.

She didn't refuse when he said he would walk her home. The morning's incident outside the hospital was still there at the back of her mind, but with sudden recklessness she decided to live for the moment.

During the downhill stroll to the headland neither of them had forgotten the small girl whose afternoon of play had turned into a helicopter ride to hospital with a possible stay in the children's orthopaedic ward ahead of her.

'Which one of us is going to phone the hospital tomorrow?' Lucas said.

'I will,' she offered. 'We haven't got a name, but I'm sure A and E will remember the little girl who arrived by helicopter. It's been quite a day, hasn't it?'

It was an opening, a chance for him to mention what he'd been doing at the hospital with his ex-fiancée, but it fell on stony ground, and when they reached Four Winds House he said, 'Thanks for coming to visit. I'll see you on Monday afternoon at my clinic and in the morning at the surgery too, as I'll be filling in for Ethan while he's away.'

'Yes, so I believe,' she said, and waited to see what he would do next.

She didn't have to wait long. 'Until Monday, then,' he told her, bent and kissed her cheek, and was gone.

Tracing her fingers across the place where his mouth had rested, she realised just how much she had fallen in love with him, and wondered if this was as far as they were ever going to get.

CHAPTER FIVE

I**T WAS** Monday morning and Meredith from the Mariners Mooring guest house had come to hear the results of the tests that Ethan had organised on her behalf, leaving Lucas with the task of telling her that the ESR test for polymyalgia had come back positive and that she needed to take some steroids.

'I don't want to have a moon face or put on lots of weight,' she wailed when she heard the news.

He'd been seeing patients since seven o'clock, mostly people who needed to see a doctor before going to work, and at eight o'clock young Maria had brought him coffee and toast, but he'd put it to one side until he'd seen Meredith, and in the light of her protest had explained to her that there was an upside to that kind of medication.

'You will have lots of energy while on the prednisolone,' he told her, 'and can take comfort that the other side effects you mentioned will be a temporary thing. They will recede once the steroids are gradually reduced in keeping with regular ESR tests.'

Meredith had left in a less fraught state of mind than when she'd arrived and at the point of departing had said on a different matter, 'You have a new doctor joining the practice today, I believe, Dr Leo Fenchurch. On Ethan's recommendation he's booked in with us for a while until he gets settled, so I'd better get back to the guest house and make sure that all is ready for his arrival.'

After she'd gone Lucas glanced through the window and was relieved to see that the red sports car was parked outside, so it seemed as if Jenna was happy enough to use it during working hours, and recalling her changing moods of Saturday he wondered what she would be like today and whether she was as uncomplicated as he'd first thought.

After the unsettling meeting with Philippa, who was very mistaken if she had any ideas about taking up where they'd left off, he'd been looking forward to Jenna's serenity and it hadn't been there. She'd had something on her mind but hadn't been prepared to say what.

Yet she'd seemed tranquil enough when she'd rung briefly on Sunday morning to report that the little girl from the accident on the rocks had sustained a fractured leg, but, apart from much bruising, had escaped any serious injury to her back.

The call had lasted only minutes as she'd been helping her mother to get dressed and as they'd said goodbye he'd been reckoning up the hours to when he would see her again.

The tea was going cold and the toast beginning to look like cardboard so he took a quick break before the new doctor arrived.

Afterwards Lucas went to the nurses' room with the notes of a patient who was due for vaccinations before a visit to the Middle East and found Jenna her usual smiling self, trim and capable as she and the other two nurses dealt with those requiring their services.

'Hello,' she said in a low voice when he appeared beside her. 'You must feel as if you've done a day's work already.'

'This is peanuts compared to a sixteen-hour shift in Theatre,' he told her whimsically.

'No wonder you're not missing it,' she commented, and before he had the chance to reply said, 'Has the new doctor arrived yet?'

'Not yet. He rang earlier to say that he's motoring down from Manchester after being on the wards until late last night, so he can be forgiven if he arrives somewhat jaded. But once he's settled in, his presence will be most welcome. Being a doctor short since Francine went hasn't made our lives any easier.'

On that observation he returned to his own room and as the morning progressed Jenna felt that the summer sun had never shone brighter because she was back near Lucas again.

* * *

When Leo Fenchurch presented himself at the surgery in the middle of the morning there was nothing jaded about his appearance. A fair-haired six-footer with a smiley mouth, his manner gave no indication of exhaustion or the guarded approach of someone in strange surroundings.

He had arrived without any luggage and when he and Lucas had introduced themselves the newcomer explained that he'd stopped off at the guest house first so that he could deposit his belongings before reporting to the surgery.

The next step was introducing Leo to the staff, which in Ethan's absence was made up of Lucas himself, the three practice nurses, three receptionists, an Age Concern representative, Brenda the cleaner, and a midwife and a district nurse who at the time of his arrival were both out on the district.

By the end of the day the older staff members were wanting to mother the new doctor and the younger ones were thinking along different lines but were just as impressed, with the exception of Jenna, who had eyes only for one man and it wasn't Leo.

Fortunately there were not many patients booked in for the heart clinic in the afternoon and as Jenna did any ECGs that Lucas required and made sure that results from other tests he'd requested were on his desk as each patient was shown into his consulting room, the afternoon passed smoothly enough, but she couldn't help thinking again that the top cardiovascular surgeon from Hunters Hill should be back where he belonged.

Yet each time the thought came, the scar across his chest would come to mind, along with a vision of the woman who had been in his life long before *she'd* appeared on the scene.

The new doctor had been familiarising himself with the layout of the practice while they'd been occupied and settling himself into the consulting room that would be his, and when it was time for the late afternoon surgery he and Lucas took it between them.

There'd been a phone call from Ethan to ask if

Leo Fenchurch had arrived and he'd been informed that he had. When Lucas had enquired how things were at his end, it sounded as if they weren't any better, and Jenna wondered what could have gone wrong between the good-natured head of the practice and his lovely French wife.

It was time to go. Most of the staff had gone and, on the point of leaving herself, Jenna asked the newcomer, 'How has your first day gone, Dr Fenchurch?'

'Fine,' he said. 'This place is something else. I'm going to like Bluebell Cove. If I don't fall asleep over my evening meal I shall have a stroll down to the beach and investigate the pub, in that order. What do you do with *your* evenings, Nurse Balfour?'

'Not a lot,' she told him laughingly. 'And my name is Jenna.'

At that moment Lucas appeared, ready to lock up for the night, and when he saw her smiling and relaxed with the new doctor, he thought grimly that this was the kind of guy who would make her happy, a carefree, easy-going type, not much unlike Ronnie the lifeguard, and totally different from himself, with his scarred body and shattered faith in the decency of others.

When Jenna arrived home her mother's first words were, 'What is the new doctor like?' Her daughter had told her that there was to be another new face at the surgery and anything of that nature was of interest to her.

'Bright and breezy, free and easy,' she replied. 'And already in love with Bluebell Cove.'

'Is he married?'

'I don't know. He's staying at Meredith's and hasn't brought anyone with him as far as I know.'

'What does Dr Devereux think of him?'

Jenna was smiling. 'I don't know. He isn't likely to confide in me, is he? I'm another newcomer and a part-time employee at that. Lucas Devereux is at the top of the hierarchy and I'm at the bottom.'

'Yes, but you *are* a Balfour.'

She took her mother's swollen hand in hers and said gently, 'The only Balfour that mattered was you…and you won't ever be forgotten.'

Her father, who had just come in from the garden, had heard what she'd said and commented, 'Jenna is right, my dear, you won't be forgotten.'

'Not by my patients maybe,' she said wryly, 'but what about the two of you who so often had to take second place?'

'We've coped, haven't we?' he said, turning to his daughter, and with the memory coming to mind of how he had once said that some day he would explain why her mother had always been so driven by her vocation, Jenna went to start preparing the evening meal with the intention of reminding him of that promise before the night was over.

The opportunity came when they were in the kitchen together, clearing away after the meal, and her mother was in the sitting room watching television. She said, 'You never did tell me why Mum was so obsessed with the practice.'

'Yes, I know. Do you want to hear it now?' he said, and she nodded.

'Her father's lifelong ambition was to be a doctor, but he came from a large family. There was never any money for that sort of thing and by the time there was he was too old to contemplate it.

'So he transferred his dream onto your mother. Was determined to realise it through her abilities, and every penny he had was swallowed up in sending her to medical school. He died on the day she got her degree, but not before he'd heard her promise that she would never let him down, that her career would come before everything else in her life, and as we both know she kept her word.'

'Why didn't you tell me this before?' she asked tearfully.

'She wouldn't let me. It is only of late that she has admitted to herself that he asked too much of her.'

* * *

There was to be a meeting in the community centre later in the evening about the forthcoming Harvest of the Sea festival, which was to take place on the first Sunday in September, in two weeks' time.

The harbourmaster would be there with the various helpers, along with those who would be taking part, and when Jenna arrived there was a general feeling of anticipation amongst them.

The sheds would be cleaned the night before the ceremony and the walls draped with fishnets. Shells and other sea ornaments, lobster pots and seaweed would be on display around a small stage that would have been erected for the sea queen and her retinue, who would appear as the first hymn was being announced by the vicar.

It was always the same one, the age-old words asking for a blessing and a safe return for those whose livelihoods depended on the sea.

When the service was over the sea queen and her attendants would proceed slowly down a centre aisle and once they had left those present would make their way to the community centre where fish and chips would be served.

The Harvest of the Sea brought many visitors to Bluebell Cove and it was always late at night before it settled back into its usual tranquillity.

When the meeting was over and it had been established that the sea queen and her retinue would indeed be wearing the straw hats and aprons in complete contrast to last year's performers who *had* slithered along as ethereal-looking mermaids, Jenna began to walk home beneath gathering thunderclouds. Within minutes jagged flashes of lightning were zig-zagging across the sky, followed almost immediately by torrential rain.

There were properties dotted along most of the road that led to the headland but there was nowhere nearby to shelter at that particular moment. Within minutes she was drenched and when a car passed her and then stopped a few feet away she prayed that it might be someone she knew.

It was, and not only that, it was the one person

she wanted to see. Lucas opened the door and ran towards her as another stroke of lightning set a tree in a nearby field on fire.

'Come on!' he cried above the noise of the elements. 'Let's get out of this.' He grabbed her hand and within seconds they were in the car and he was turning it round and heading back to the village.

'Where are we going?' she asked, with hair soaked and rivulets of rain running down her face.

'Away from that lot,' he said grimly. 'The worst of the storm is in the direction that you were going and you saw what it did to that tree, didn't you?'

She nodded, her teeth beginning to chatter as the dress she was wearing clung to her like an extra skin.

Lucas was pulling up outside The Old Chart House and said, 'In you go. You need a hot toddy and some dry clothes. This is some storm!'

'We never do things by halves on the coast,' she told him, managing a shaky smile.

'Is that a promise or a threat?' he asked dryly as he hurried her inside.

It was an hour later and the storm was still raging. Jenna had phoned home to let her parents know she was all right and was sheltering at Dr Devereux's house. 'I'll be with you as soon as it slackens off,' she'd told her father as she'd sat sipping the hot toddy that Lucas had promised her.

He'd found her a robe from somewhere to put on while her clothes dried, an expensive satin creation, and it wasn't hard to guess who it belonged to. It went against the grain having to wear it, but the alternative was sitting around in her underwear until her dress was dry, and if ever she took her clothes off for Lucas it wasn't going to be because she'd got soaked in a downpour. So the long satin number that swept the floor when she stood up would have to suffice.

She could smell perfume on it, lingering and musky, equally as exotic as the garment, and it didn't make her feel any better when Lucas appeared with a hot-water bottle.

'I've switched the heating on,' he told her, 'but it does take a little while to come through.'

'You're very kind,' she mumbled, and he laughed.

'What did you expect me to do? Hang you out on the washing line to dry?'

'No, of course not,' she said huffily, 'but you must realise that I'm at a disadvantage wearing another woman's robe and looking like a drowned rat.'

He was still amused. 'Take comfort in knowing that you look much better in it than she did, and never having seen a drowned rat I can't comment on that. But your dress will soon be dry and then you can make your escape. It's in the dryer.'

There wasn't much she could say to that so she stared into space and tried to look dignified. Lucas disappeared again and a while later he brought her the dress dried *and ironed*, and it seemed unreal that someone of his standing should be filling hot-water bottles for her and drying her clothes.

She'd discovered that he wasn't the type to

pull rank, but this was going the extra mile, or was it because finding her in the storm and bringing her back to The Old Chart House had livened up a dull evening for him? With those sorts of questions in mind she said impulsively, 'Are you lonely, Lucas?'

He sat down beside her and said softly, 'Yes, but why do you ask?'

'I don't know. It was just a thought. I guess… I get lonely too, Lucas.'

There was a moment's pause between them, a moment in which they both gazed into each other's eyes and saw the pent-up feelings and desires they held for each other. And their lips met in a warm, wonderful, passionate kiss that Jenna simply wanted to go on for ever.

When they finally parted Lucas gazed longingly into her eyes, and giving into complete recklessness she asked, 'Would you like me to sleep with you, Lucas?'

Dark brows were rising above amazed hazel eyes as he drew back, then replied, 'No. No, Jenna. And if ever I would, I will do the asking.

It's not that I don't want you, but I'm not wanting payment in kind for looking after you.'

Her colour was rising at his refusal and she said hastily, 'I'll bear that in mind. Don't worry, I won't suggest anything like that again.'

His expression had softened. Of course he wanted to sleep with her, wanted to hold her close in the night against his ravaged chest and offer up silent thanks. But he was damned if he wanted it to be because she was sorry for him.

She went upstairs to get dressed in one of the bedrooms. Not his, after the faux pas she'd just made, and when she reappeared he said, 'Where had you been when I picked you up?'

'There'd been a meeting about the Harvest of the Sea in the community centre. You're not going to come, are you?'

'Why not? Is it tickets only and they're all sold?' he joked.

'No, of course not!' she exclaimed, relieved that his good humour was restored. 'It's a church-type service.'

'So why don't you want me to come?'

'Because of me?'

'But that's the reason why I'll be there, wanting to see you in all your oceanic finery.'

'Yes, well, don't expect a mermaid draped over a rock, brushing her hair.'

He could have told her that no matter what she was appearing as she would be beautiful, but after the way he'd reacted to her offering to sleep with him it might not go down too well.

It was gone midnight and the storm had passed. A harvest moon was shining in a cloudless sky as Lucas drove Jenna home. There was silence in the car, each occupied with their own thoughts, but they were brought back to reality when they reached the headland as all the house lights were on at Four Winds, and the moment he pulled up on the drive her father was at the door, his voice taut with anxiety.

'Thank God you've come with Jenna, Dr Devereux!' he exclaimed. 'Her mother isn't well and says she suspects she's having a heart attack. I was about to ring for an ambulance when I heard you pull up.'

Lucas felt his chest muscles tighten, but they were both out of the car in a flash and he said to her father, 'Take me to her, Mr Balfour.'

Barbara was in bed propped up with pillows and breathing heavily. Her lips were blue and frothy and he asked, 'Where is the pain, Dr Balfour?'

'In the middle like a heavy weight,' she gasped.

He turned to Jenna. 'Will you fetch my case out of the car while I phone for an ambulance?' To her mother he said, 'I'm going to check your heartbeat and pulse rate. You are almost certainly having a myocardial infarction.' He turned to her anxious husband. 'A heart attack, Mr Balfour. Could you find an extra blanket as your wife feels cold and very clammy.'

As he examined Barbara, Lucas thought he'd seen patients in this state countless times and prayed that there wasn't sorrow ahead for Jenna and her father. There wouldn't be if he could help it. Whatever dark moments might plague him, this was his world, and if anybody could save Barbara, he could. Jenna was back beside him with his case, her face white with shock, and he thought that it was turning out to be some night, and speed was of the essence if he was going to be able to bring her mother through this.

It seemed as if his voice on the phone to A and E had brought results as within minutes the familiar wail of an ambulance siren could be heard in the silent night.

As it drew nearer he said to Jenna, 'See if you can persuade your father to stay here. He is very stressed but will maybe calm down now that he knows we're in charge and will be better off at home for the time being.'

'I've already suggested it,' she told him, 'and I think he's relieved not to have to make that journey in the middle of the night. So it will be just you and I with Mum in the ambulance.'

Her mother was gasping with the pain and he said gently, 'The injection I've just given you will kick in soon and there will be some relief.

The ambulance will be here in seconds and they'll have oxygen on board, and when we get there I'll take over.'

She managed a glimmer of a smile. 'I can't ask for more than that, can I?'

No one could, Jenna thought. He'd been there for her earlier in the evening, and now in these dire and stressful moments Lucas was being there for her mother.

Sadly there was no one to be there for him when he needed someone, unless the owner of the sexy satin robe was back in his life.

Surprised expressions were mixed with welcoming smiles when the staff of the coronary unit hurried forward to take charge of the new admission, with Lucas Devereux pushing the trolley. There were even more expressions of surprise when they recognised the patient as a retired GP who had always been a force to be reckoned with when it came to the welfare of her patients.

But there wasn't time for explanations and if

anyone wondered who the pale-faced woman with them was, the question was left unasked.

Mark Stephens was the consultant in charge of the unit and wouldn't normally have been present at that time of night, but there had been a few urgent admissions and he'd stayed late to check them out personally, never dreaming that his friend Lucas was going to suddenly appear from wherever he'd been hiding.

But there was no time for anything other than setting the wheels in motion to save a patient's life, and on this occasion with Lucas himself on the scene.

An ECG showed that Barbara's heart attack was severe enough but could have been worse, and when Mark Stephens had gone home to his bed Lucas took charge of Barbara's treatment while Jenna stood close by, wrapped around with dread.

It consisted, amongst other things, of intravenous fluids to prevent shock, painkillers, and thrombolitic drugs to dissolve blood clots, given to patients who have arrived in a coronary care unit within a short space of time from the onset of the attack.

By the time dawn was lightening the sky Barbara's condition was stabilising, and knowing that she would be monitored round the clock, Lucas took Jenna home for a short break.

When she'd protested that she didn't want to leave her mother, he'd told her that she would be of more use when she'd had a rest, some breakfast and reported her mother's condition to her father, and that once he'd sorted out the practice, they would go back.

'I'm afraid that Leo Fenchurch is going to feel that he's been thrown in at the deep end as he's going to be taking the morning and after-noon surgeries today,' he said as they drove the last few miles to Bluebell Cove, 'but after seeing him perform yesterday I'm sure he will cope, and Lucy and Maria will have to manage without you too.'

She nodded, fighting off exhaustion, and he wanted to take her in his arms and tell her it was going to be all right, but first he had to make sure that it wasn't an empty promise. Her mother was responding to the treatment so far, but if it turned out that surgery *was* required, *he* would do it, and the tightness in his chest was back.

As Four Winds House came in sight she said soberly, 'You might find it hard to believe, Lucas, but it is only since she became ill and had to retire that I'm getting to know my mother, and now I might lose her.' There were tears on her lashes and he stopped the car by the side of the road.

'Come here,' he said gently, holding out his arms, and she wept out her anxiety against the scarred chest that she'd once seen uncovered. When she had no more tears left he fished out a box of tissues from the glove compartment and said quietly, 'Tell me, Jenna. Who am I?'

'The best for heart surgery,' she snuffled, sitting reluctantly upright.

He smiled. 'Not necessarily, but I do know my job. We'll be back at the hospital soon, and if your mother carries on responding as she is there may be no need for surgery, but if there is…'

'You'll do it,' she whispered.

'You can bet on it.'

'And then they'll persuade you to go back and take up where you left off.'

'I alone will know when I'm ready for that, and it won't be yet as Ethan needs me at the moment. He was there for me when I was at rock bottom and I want to be there for him during this awful divorce business.'

She'd phoned her father with the details of her mother's progress and told him that they were on their way home for a short break. When they arrived he had breakfast ready, and when they'd eaten he listened intently to what they had to say about his wife.

The clock was on seven when they'd finished and Lucas said, 'I'm off to the surgery to make sure they can manage, and will be back shortly. OK?'

'Yes. Have I time for a shower?' she asked, realising that she hadn't washed or put a comb through her hair since being caught in the storm.

'If you're quick,' he replied, and off he went.

He was back in half an hour with the news that while he'd been there Ethan had phoned and when he'd heard about her mother's heart attack and the effect it was having on the staffing of the surgery he'd said that he was going to take the first flight back and would visit his children again some time soon when the situation had been resolved.

When Jenna and Lucas arrived at the hospital the second time, Barbara was still responding to the treatment and he gave a satisfied smile. Mark Stephens was back on duty after a brief respite, and as the two consultants discussed her mother's condition Jenna held her hand tightly.

'Is Keith all right?' she asked faintly.

'Yes, he's fine,' she told her. 'Very concerned about you but holding the fort at home. He made us a lovely breakfast and sends his love. It won't be long before he appears just to make sure that you are doing as well as Lucas says you are.'

'I might need surgery, you know. Will he be prepared to operate if I do?'

'Yes, but if you carry on as you are it won't be the life-threatening sort, more of a remedial nature. They are going to get you through this. You are a legend in this place, you know. They call you Battling Barbara.'

'Maybe if I'd done a little less of that I might be a fitter woman now,' her mother remarked dryly, 'but we have to go where our hearts lead us, Jenna, and just in case I don't come through this I want you to know that I'm proud of you, so proud. I was a good doctor, but left a lot to be desired as a mother. I don't know how you and your father have put up with me.'

'Just get better,' she said softly. 'That is all Dad and I want.'

'I'll do my best,' she promised, and drifted off to sleep.

'What's the verdict?' Jenna asked when Lucas came to stand beside her.

'Good, and not so good,' he replied. 'Your mother has had more tests while we've been absent and they've shown that there is fluid in the lungs, which is often brought on by heart failure, so I've suggested we put her on diuretic medication for that, and beta-blocker drugs to reduce any risk of further damage to the heart muscle. So she's not quite out of danger yet, but we're getting there. At the moment I'm not considering surgery of any kind, but will be keeping a close eye on her progress and if I feel there is the slightest need of it, I will have her in Theatre immediately.'

She was still sleeping, hadn't heard the conversation, and Jenna thought it was amazing that her mother was so compliant on finding herself to be the patient instead of the doctor.

CHAPTER SIX

THERE was consternation when the people in Bluebell Cove heard that their much-loved doctor was in hospital, and during the next few days the number of visitors had to be limited as half the village wanted to visit and Lucas was adamant that Barbara needed rest and quiet.

Keith was with her most of the time and Jenna came and went as her working hours allowed, now that her mother was out of danger. The medication that Lucas and Mark Stephens had ordered seemed to be working, and by the weekend the patient was out of bed and taking short strolls in the hospital gardens beneath the watchful eyes of the coronary staff.

Every time Jenna thought about the night of the storm it was with disbelief that so much could have happened in so short a time, and when she remembered the part that Lucas had played both in rescuing her from the deluge and being there for her during her mother's heart attack, she sent up a prayer of thanks.

But every time she tried to express her gratitude it was as if he didn't want to know and preferred to adopt the businesslike manner he'd had when they'd first met. So as the days passed she retreated behind a barrier of her own made up of a distant sort of politeness, and wept in her pillow every night for the futility of her love for him.

Her mother was discharged in the middle of the following week and life began to return slowly to normal. Ethan suggested that Jenna take as long as she needed to look after her, but even though Barbara was mellowing, the practice still came first in her life and she insisted that she and Keith could cope during the short time that Jenna was working at the surgery.

Lucas called frequently to check her over and Jenna thought dolefully that her parents were seeing more of him than she was. With Ethan back and Leo there to assist, Lucas wasn't needed any more during surgery hours except for his two heart clinics, and while she was assisting on those occasions they spoke only of medical matters, to the extent that she began to feel she must have imagined the closeness they'd shared previously.

On his part Lucas was keeping a tight hold on his feelings. He knew Jenna was grateful for all that he'd done for them that night, but he didn't want any offers like the one she'd made when he'd brought her in from the storm and had admitted he was lonely.

She'd offered to sleep with him then, he felt, out of pity, and the last thing he wanted was a repeat performance of it out of gratitude. So he was keeping her at arm's length and feeling totally miserable in the process, until he heard someone mention that it was the Harvest of the Sea on the coming Sunday and he remembered he'd said he would be there. But it would be a matter of a seat at the back and a quick exit when the ceremony was over.

As the week progressed Ethan said that he would be going and that they might as well go together to see Jenna and the rest of those taking part, and for lack of an excuse he agreed to go with his friend to the fish-and-chip supper afterwards.

He wasn't expecting the festival to be anything special but his eyes widened when he and Ethan entered the largest gutting shed, which was always used for the occasion. Fishing nets hung gracefully from the ceiling and were draped along the whitewashed walls, and there were lots of pictures of the sea in tranquil mode and in fury.

Smooth white pebbles and prettily coloured shells were scattered along the sides of the room amidst an assortment of lobster pots and life belts, and at the front there was a small stage.

The place was full to capacity and as an organist, tucked away in a corner, began to play a sea shanty the door behind the congregation opened and everyone got to their feet as the sea queen appeared, carrying a large silver cod on a platter, and began to walk slowly towards the stage with her four attendants following in single file.

As he watched Lucas was smiling. Now he understood Jenna's reservations about the outfit. Yet it was so right for the occasion. With the flat straw boater, the dark blue apron with its broad white stripes, and the shapeless waterproof shoes on her feet, she looked as he'd known she would, quite beautiful.

He tried to catch her attention but either on purpose or unknowingly she never looked in his direction and he thought wryly that he'd asked for that. Having been the cool consultant for the last couple of weeks, calling her 'Nurse', as if he didn't know her name, she was hardly going to beam at him over the heads of the assembled throng.

She walked carefully up the steps and seated herself on a throne-like chair in the centre of the stage and one by one her attendants came to stand beside her.

Once they were in position the vicar said a word of welcome to those present and the organist struck up with the sailor's hymn 'Eternal Father Strong to Save' and the rafters of the fish shed rang with the plea for safe passage for those who sailed the seas.

The first lesson was read by a coastguard from the station on a rise above the harbour and the second by a member of the crew of the lifeboat. Then it was time for the sea queen to be crowned, and as Jenna held the glistening cod high in the air Lucas was amazed to see Barbara walking slowly up the steps that led to the stage, with a committee member assisting her on either side. When she removed the hat from Jenna's head and replaced it with a crown made of sea shells then planted a kiss on her brow, there wasn't a dry eye in the place.

He tried to find the sea queen when it was over but she was nowhere to be seen amongst the crowd, so he followed Ethan into the community hall where the meal was being served and discovered her serving fish and chips to the masses with the crown of shells still on her head.

She'd seen him come in and nodded briefly in

his direction between scooping out a portion of chips on to a plate beside a piece of delicious-looking fried fish and presenting it to the first person in the queue.

By the time he and Ethan were due to be served, a silver-haired old lady had taken over and Jenna was nowhere to be seen again. When he'd finished eating he told his friend he was going to find her and Ethan showed no surprise, which made Lucas think so much for keeping his feelings under wraps in that quarter.

She was on the beach, as he'd guessed she would be, seated on a rock, watching the tide come in as she'd done a thousand times before, and when he said her name she turned slowly to face him without speaking.

'The service was lovely,' he said in a low voice, 'and so were you. The costumes were just right for the occasion, though I see that you've changed out of yours already. Why?'

'I smelt of fish, cod to be precise, but I'm pleased that the service made sense to you,' she replied flatly.

'Of course it did!' he exclaimed. 'Why shouldn't it have? It was very moving, and when I saw your mother making her way slowly up those steps I was amazed that she'd found the strength to do it.'

She nodded. 'I didn't know she was going to do that, but the organisers had asked her to and Mum can't resist a challenge. She went straight to bed when she got home, though. I helped her get settled and Dad is with her now.'

'I think I should call and take a look at her just to make sure she hasn't overdone it,' he suggested. 'Are you coming?'

'I'll follow on. I'm sure you don't need *me* around.'

Not much! he thought as she went on to say, 'Your giving me the cold shoulder is because I offered to sleep with you, isn't it? Don't you see that it was because I care about you?'

'You mean you're sorry for me because I've got a cut on my chest and I made an error of judgement in my choice of a fiancée?'

'Yes, if that's what you want to think. But maybe you've become reconciled.'

'Reconciled!' he hooted. 'Of course we haven't. Wherever did you get that idea from?'

'I saw you with her on the day that I took Mum and Lucy shopping. You were on the point of going into the hospital together.'

'Yes, and you came to the wrong conclusion. Philippa was over for a family wedding and had gone to Hunters Hill to look up old acquaintances, and I'd gone to pick up some clothes that I'd left there. Our grand reunion lasted just five minutes.'

'I see,' she said, with a lift to her voice at the explanation for one of the things that had been bugging her, and as for the other, if Lucas was insisting that it was he who would take the initiative in moving on their relationship, *or otherwise,* she would at least be aware of the true state of his feelings when it happened, if it ever did, and instead of leaving him to go up to the house alone she fell into step beside him.

Her mother was asleep and looked frail but peaceful as they stood looking down at her, and

Jenna said tonelessly, 'There is more to come, isn't there, Lucas? We can't sit back and relax with regard to Mum's health problems.'

'No, you can't, I'm afraid,' he replied. 'When she gets a little stronger we might try angioplasty to improve the heart muscle, but it will have to be done soon, and as for the arthritis treatment she's on, it can't be bettered. Just live one day at a time, Jenna, and count your blessings.'

He put a finger under her chin and lifting her face to his said, 'You know where to find me if you need me. I won't ever be far away, and now I'm going to say goodnight to your father and then call it a day.'

'I won't ever be far away,' Lucas had said, and as Jenna lay sleepless in her room with the familiar sound of the sea in her ears, she was hugging the thought to her. There was joy in it, comfort, and a feeling of promise that was making her uncertainties seem foolish.

* * *

As September progressed, with its summer days and darker nights and fruit ready for picking on the trees, it was time for the harvest of the land to be gathered in by the farmers around Bluebell Cove.

The mantle of autumn had fallen upon the village, with the trees shaking off their leaves into carpets of gold and bronze, blackberries glistening on wayside bushes, and the elusive wind berries lying low in dark abundance beside the gorse.

At the biggest farm in the area there was always a celebratory ball when the harvesting was done, and an invitation was always sent to the surgery. It was an occasion that no one liked to miss as good food was always on offer and barrels of Devon cider were on hand to quench thirst.

The owner of Wheatlands Farm was Jack Enderby, and his father George was one of Lucas's patients at his heart clinic. When the invitations were being sent out, the old man asked that one should be sent to his doctor.

'It's the guy who got stabbed by the relative of a patient,' he told Jack, 'and he's moved out here to get away from it all for a while.'

His son was suitably impressed but commented that he would be included in the general invitation to everyone at the surgery, wouldn't he?

'Nay, he's a separate item,' his father said, and so consequently Lucas came to the nurses' room one morning to ask if Jenna knew anything about the invitation he'd received.

'I know where it has come from,' she told him. 'The Enderbys have a very large farm and have a ball with a band and all the trimmings when the harvest is in. It's evening dress as it is a very upmarket occasion.

'They always send an invitation to the surgery, but for some reason they've sent yours separately. It's perhaps because George Enderby, father of the guy who owns the place, is one of your patients. So are you going to accept?'

If he said no it would ruin her night as the dark brooding look was there again, but his reply was reassuring. 'Of course, *if you'll be my partner.*' And as an afterthought added, 'That is, if you aren't already spoken for.'

She could have told him that she might have been 'spoken for' quite easily, as she'd refused three invitations from very presentable members of the community, but why bother? He was the one she wanted to be with, so she told him casually, 'No. I'm free.'

'Good.' He gazed down at the invitation in his hand. 'The last time I went out socially was with Philippa. It was the night we split up after I'd given her her marching orders.' He smiled a mirthless smile. 'She never did like being put in her place.' And, as if that was the end of that, he went on, 'I see that the ball is this coming Saturday so I'll pick you up around eightish, if that's all right?'

'Yes, that will be fine,' she agreed, and off he went, leaving her to wonder once again just how deep his hurts went.

Lucy had appeared at that moment and when he'd gone she said, 'Am I right in thinking that love is in the air?'

Jenna sighed. 'Frustration maybe, or indecision, but I'm not sure about love.'

'You mean because Lucas isn't chasing you?' the elderly nurse questioned dryly.

'Yes, I suppose that's what I mean,' she said dejectedly. 'He will have asked me to go with him because it's convenient. He knows me, knows I'm not in any kind of a relationship, because I'm so attracted to *him*, so he probably thinks I'll fill the gap nicely.'

'Has it occurred to you that you might be wrong about that?' Lucy questioned. 'Lucas Devereux is a man of principle. It could be that he doesn't want you to think he's on the rebound and out to take advantage of you.

'Did you know that he's refused to press charges against the man who almost killed him? In my book that is forgiveness beyond belief. So think about it, my dear.'

'Yes, I will,' she said slowly. She would think long and hard.

Life at the practice was carrying on as normal, with Leo Fenchurch settling in with breezy confidence, Ethan giving no sign of the heartache that the thought of divorce was bringing, and Lucas available if needed, but otherwise taking just the two heart clinics while he recharged his batteries.

Amongst the nursing staff normality was mixed with Maria having a teenage crush on Dr. Fenchurch, Lucy talking about retiring, and Jenna on an emotional see-saw every time she was near Lucas. His promise not to be far away from her all the time was the upside of it, but would he ever say the words she longed to hear?

He had performed balloon angioplasty on her mother's heart to increase the flow of blood through a narrowed valve and there was an improvement in her condition. 'It might have to be done again in a year or so,' he'd told Barbara, 'but that would be no problem.'

'I consider myself very fortunate that you have my interests at heart, Dr Devereux,' Barbara had told him in her precise way when she'd been discharged from hospital after the treatment, and taking him by surprise had questioned, 'Does the same apply to my daughter? Do you have *her* interests at heart? If you have, I will die happy.'

He'd smiled. 'Whether I have or not, you are not going to die yet, Dr Balfour. I wouldn't have said that a few weeks ago but you are reacting well to the angioplasty.'

Jenna had appeared at that moment and the conversation had hung in the air, giving her the feeling of being talked about, and if that *was* the case her mother and Lucas hadn't seemed inclined to tell her what it was about.

After the staid outfit she'd worn for the Harvest of the Sea she was determined that her dress for the ball at Wheatlands Farm was going to make up for it. The colours she looked best in were cream, blue, some shades of green, *and black*, and black it was going to be.

The magazine of Hunters Hill Hospital was still in the glove compartment of the sports car, and even though Lucas had been emphatic that it was all over between the flame-haired woman and himself, Jenna felt inadequate every time she observed the other woman's elegance.

The little black number she'd picked up in Italy would be just the thing to impress him if that was what he was used to, and it would give her the confidence she needed to be Lucas's partner.

On the night of the ball her mother stayed up later than usual so that she could see her set off with him, and when Jenna came downstairs, looking beautiful and sophisticated, she took her father's breath away, and her mother nodded her approval.

The dress was long with a sweeping skirt that had diamanté along the hemline. It was clinging, strapless with a low-cut bodice. The most sophisticated thing she'd ever bought.

She'd swept her hair up in a long golden swathe that was held in position with a jewelled comb, and when Lucas pulled up on the drive in the black Mercedes that was *his* choice of transport she went to let him in with eyes bright with anticipation.

He was in evening dress and looked cool and

unruffled as he presented her with a corsage of white roses. 'I didn't know what you'd be wearing,' he said, 'so white seemed to be the safest choice.'

'They're lovely,' she breathed.

'And so are you,' he said in a low voice, and went on, as his glance took in the dress, 'Is there going to be anywhere you can fasten the corsage? There isn't much fabric around your shoulders. How about wearing it at your waist?'

'Or in my hair. I'll go and fix it. Mum and Dad are in the sitting room if you want a word.'

'Yes, sure,' he agreed, and looking tall, trim, every inch a man who was rising above pain and betrayal and keeping his own integrity, he went to find them.

He hadn't exactly been bursting with admiration when he'd seen her outfit, Jenna thought. All right, he'd said she was beautiful, but the only comment he'd made about her dress had been the lack of it around her neck and shoulders, so when they were driving between the hedgerows to the Enderbys' farm she asked casually, 'Do you like my dress?'

He took his glance off the road for a second, observed her expression, and replied, 'Yes, of course. It's just that I'm used to seeing you in sunshine colours, blues, greens and gold. Philippa used to wear a lot of...'

'Black?'

'Yes.'

'And?'

He was smiling. 'And nothing. She lacked your radiance that lights up even the darkest of colours.'

She wasn't feeling very radiant after *that* conversation, Jenna thought.

Why had she been so stupid as to try to copy the seductive stance that Philippa's body line had conveyed when she'd seen them outside the hospital, and also in the magazine, which was beginning to appear well fingered?

'I suppose you'd rather see me in something like the outfit I wore that night in the fish sheds,' she said.

He pulled over to the side of the road and

turned towards her. 'Jenna,' he said softly, 'I told you that you were beautiful when I arrived, and meant it, but obviously you feel that I'm not playing the part you have mapped out for me. If it is still rankling because I didn't take you up on your offer to sleep with me, it was because I once went into a relationship with eyes wide open, yet was too blind to see what was in front of me.'

'Maybe this will go a little way towards making up for what I said that night.' Her eyes widened as he reached across and kissed her long and lingeringly until she was limp and gasping from the kind of sexual chemistry that previously she'd only dreamt about.

When he moved away and eased himself back behind the steering-wheel, she sat without speaking and remained like that until Lucas pulled onto the parking area at the farm, which was already full of cars, and turned towards her once more. But this time it was to say, 'Am I forgiven, or have I made things worse?'

She was smiling, and he thought how lovely

she was in spite of the overly sophisticated dress. He would probably be the only man there who thought it was. But to him Jenna was like a cleansing spirit who was wiping away the hurts that had come his way and she was right, he did prefer the straw hat and the rest of her sea queen outfit, no matter how ridiculous that might seem.

The farmhouse was huge, the barns and other outbuildings in immaculate condition. The whole place spoke of wealth and expertise, but there was no indication of that in the friendliness with which the Enderbys were greeting their guests. They were obviously well pleased that once again they were holding the ball that celebrated the gathering in of the harvest.

There were lanterns hanging from the trees in the garden and beneath them was a bar and chairs and tables, and inside the huge room where the dancing was to take place there was another bar and more lanterns.

When Jenna and Lucas appeared, George

Enderby came across the room to shake them by the hand, and then one after the other asked about her mother and welcomed to the village the newcomer who was her partner for the evening.

Ronnie the lifeguard was there with his family, and young Maria was watching the door to see if Leo, the new doctor, was going to appear, but Jenna thought sympathetically she might be in for a disappointment as they'd seen him driving in the opposite direction on their way to the ball.

She had recovered from the disappointment of Lucas not being impressed with her dress. His explanation had soothed her wounded pride. *And that kiss!*

She'd wanted it to go on for ever, even though he'd given no indication of anything changing permanently between them, but the night was young and so was she. She was here to enjoy herself with the man of her dreams.

It was like coming home after a long journey, Lucas was thinking, and all because of the woman by his side. She was the reason why he wasn't rushing to go back to the cut and thrust of the big hospital. He would have to eventually, of course, he owed it to his calling, but magical evenings like this with Jenna were too precious to pass by, just as afternoons spent with her in his heart clinic were equally special.

The weather that sometimes changed with the tides was being kind. It was a mellow autumn evening with a veritable banquet waiting to be eaten in the interval when the dancing stopped, and most of it came from the fields and livestock of the farm.

Midnight had been and gone. Dawn was breaking when revellers began to drift away and the band began to pack up their instruments, and shortly afterwards Jenna and Lucas said their goodbyes to the Enderbys and drove out into the silence of the early morning.

They had to pass The Old Chart House before reaching the headland, and she waited to see if Lucas would suggest they stop off there, but he drove straight past and when they were clear of it said, 'Why don't we go down to the beach and swim in the dawn? We can get changed behind the rocks.'

She was observing him in amazement. 'I haven't got a costume.'

'We'll be parking near Four Winds,' he said, unperturbed. 'Can't you creep in and change into one without disturbing your parents?'

'Er, yes, I suppose I could.' She was warming to the idea with every second. 'What about you, though?'

'I've got some swimming trunks in the boot that I carry around just in case I see those snowy white breakers and am tempted.'

By the time she'd gone into the house and changed into the bikini that she'd been wearing the first time she'd seen him, Lucas had changed in the car and was waiting for her to appear.

They had it all to themselves, the sea, the sand and the pearly dawn making a perfect ending to a wonderful night. And as they frolicked and laughed as each wave hit them Jenna's mind wasn't on the dangerous rip tides that even many experienced swimmers found themselves helpless against, challenging them to get back to dry land and safety.

But she was reminded of them when she felt the frightening pull beneath her and cried out in alarm. Lucas was bobbing beside her in a matter of seconds and they fought the rip tide together, his strength mainly responsible for pulling them away from the current to safer water. Seconds later they collapsed onto the sand and as they did so she burst into tears.

'Don't cry,' he said, putting his arms around her. 'It's all right, Jenna, you're safe.'

'Yes, I know,' she wailed, 'but I've been swimming on this beach all my life and I've seen what a rip tide can do. You are a stranger to it and could have drowned because of me.'

'But I didn't and neither did you,' he consoled. 'And you're shivering.'

He went and brought a beach towel from the car and wrapping it round her said, 'Slip your costume off beneath the towel and dry yourself a bit. Then I'm going to take you for a hot drink.'

'There won't be anywhere open at this hour,' she protested, 'and I don't want to go into the house and have Mum and Dad catch me in this state.'

'I'm taking you to my place so don't worry. A hot bath and some breakfast is what you need and then I'll take you home.'

'All right,' she agreed meekly, aware that it had taken a scare in a rip tide to get an invitation to visit his house again, but she was being ungrateful. If Lucas hadn't been there she might have succumbed, and that would have been the end of that.

She'd had a bath and came downstairs to the appetising smell of bacon grilling, and this time Lucas had found her one of his robes to wear instead of the seductive satin number.

Needless to say, it buried her and did nothing for her sex appeal. Trying not to smile, he said, 'This is the second time I've brought you in from the wet, isn't it? Maybe I should turn this place into a home for waifs and strays instead of consulting rooms.'

He pointed to the chairs around the kitchen table and said, 'Take a seat.'

She did as he asked and he placed tea, toast, and egg and bacon in front of her and said, 'Would you agree that the night has been eventful? That fantastic ball, the beach at daybreak, the rip tide treacherous and unexpected, and now this.'

What he meant by 'this' she wasn't sure, but there was one thing that she *was* sure of. Amongst the happenings of the night had been *the kiss* and it hadn't received a mention.

In the middle of eating the last piece of toast she fell asleep and, lifting her up into his arms, he carried her carefully upstairs and laid her on his bed. As he stood looking down at her he was remembering how she'd offered to sleep with him because he'd admitted he was lonely.

He placed a blanket over her and as she slept on went downstairs. As he began to clear away the breakfast things, he tried to think of a good reason to explain why he was going to be taking the Balfours' daughter home in a bathrobe and a bikini when she'd left the night before in all her finery.

CHAPTER SEVEN

IT WAS late morning when Jenna awoke. For the
first few seconds she wondered where she was,
but light soon dawned. The robe she was
wearing, finding herself in the room where
Lucas slept and the sight of her bikini hung over
the back of a chair soon had her sitting upright.

She sighed. He must have carried her upstairs
and laid her on his bed. It was typical of the way
their relationship was developing that she'd been
in his arms but had been so deeply asleep she
hadn't known anything about it.

But now it was midday and she needed some
clean clothes and an explanation ready regarding her overdue return from the ball in a bikini
if her parents were around, *and it wasn't going
to be that she'd lost a glass slipper*, though in her

present state she could easily double for Cinderella in the days before her luck changed.

Footsteps on the stairs told her that Lucas was approaching and seconds later he was framed in the doorway. On seeing that she was awake, he came and perched beside her on the bed and as he looked down at her she moaned, 'Why am I always at a disadvantage when you're around, Lucas?'

He laughed. 'I hadn't noticed.'

'Not much!' she hooted. 'Look at me now, huddled in this tent-like thing of yours. I would have been having a sedate breakfast while regaling Mum and Dad with the events of the ball if it hadn't been for the rip tide.'

'And me bringing you back here, I'm sure you're thinking.'

'Well, yes.'

'Mmm. So am I going to take you home now and present you to your parents?'

'If you must.'

'Jenna, of course I must. When you left the house last night you were in my care and still are, so if you'd like to put on the bikini and put a comb through your hair we'll be off.'

As they drove the short distance to Four Winds House she said, 'My dad is an old innocent—he won't read anything into me being out all night—but my mother misses nothing and when she sees me like this she'll be putting two and two together and making five.'

He was smiling. 'What a shame she can't add up. Everyone knows that two plus two is four.'

She was laughing across at him from the passenger seat and he thought that she would be so easy to live with, this lovely woman who was making him see everything in a different perspective.

As far as he knew, life had never hurt Jenna. She was generous and tranquil, but much as he was attracted to her he wasn't going to do anything about it until he was sure that he could make her happy.

In spite of her mother's obsession with her career, she'd been brought up in a stable home that she'd always known would be there, while he'd had to fend for himself most of the time. She'd picked up on that, with the result that she'd asked if he was lonely.

She'd drawn the line at asking him if he wanted children. Of course he did. He longed to experience the joy of holding a child of his own in his arms, but a child needed a mother and he shuddered every time he thought of the kind of mother Philippa would have been. Selfish, deceitful, it would have been a wonder if she'd found time to give him any children, with ruthless ambition souring her soul. Jenna, on the other hand...

There were no signs of life when they got to the Balfours'. No family car on the drive. No Keith pottering in the garden. When they went inside there was a note on the hall table to say that he had taken Barbara for a drive and they would be eating out. He'd ring her during the morning to make sure she had got home safely.

'So you're off the hook,' he said, 'and I'm going home to do my Sunday chores. I will see you tomorrow at the heart clinic, and, Jenna, watch for the rip tides if you go swimming without me. In fact, I might have a word with your friend Ronnie to let him know that you were nearly swept out to sea. Why wasn't he on duty?'

'He has to get some sleep. Dawn was only just breaking,' she protested. 'I was to blame. I should have been more alert, and you shouldn't have been distracting me.'

'All right, if you say so. But don't give me any more frights like that, and now I really do have to go. As well as doing some chores I have an architect coming this afternoon to advise me on the alterations I would have to make if I do decide to turn part of The Old Chart House into a private heart clinic, and I don't want to miss him. OK?'

'Of course, but before you go can I ask you something?'

He pretended to groan. 'You're not going to ask if I want to sleep with you again, are you?'

'No! I'm not!' she protested, blushing. 'And I would be obliged if you wouldn't mention that again. What I want to ask you is when are you going back to Hunters Hill? There must be sick people there who need you more than we do here.'

'Do you think I don't know that?' he said grimly. 'I don't need reminding. It isn't from choice that I'm no longer there. You above all people have seen what I'm like. How I have to psych myself up to deal with anything medically unforeseen and life-threatening. I'm all right in the clinic because I know the score. And I started it to make up for my absence at the hospital to a small degree.'

'I know you did,' she told him contritely. 'I didn't mean to upset you, Lucas. I know how difficult it is.' But he was through the door and getting into the car before she could tell him that she couldn't bear to see his expertise wasted.

As it disappeared from sight she went slowly upstairs, stripped off the bikini, and thought, So much for trying to persuade Lucas to go back to Hunters Hill. She'd stepped out of line, but with the best intentions, and if she said one word at his clinic tomorrow it would choke her.

She'd been a fool to think they might have

something precious, that they understood each other, she thought tearfully, something that usually came only once in a lifetime. The suggestion she'd made had come from love and a deep admiration.

Back at The Old Chart House Lucas was gazing bleakly out of the bedroom window, the same bedroom where Jenna had slept away her tiredness after the ball and the happenings on the beach—and where he'd been filled with tenderness as he'd gazed at her.

But what had happened to that same tenderness when she'd wanted him to go back to his position at the hospital? He'd been an absolute pain and blown his top. She'd been right, of course. He was well again in body and mind and should be thinking about returning.

Maybe without realising it, guilt had been building up inside him and he'd been using his concern for Ethan as an excuse for putting off going back to the place where he'd almost died at the hands of the distraught relative of a patient, *and had also been faced with deception beyond belief.*

But Jenna's clear thinking had brought his reluctance out into the open and, instead of thanking her for doing so, he'd berated her as if she'd done something wrong.

Tomorrow he would make things right with Jenna, again, and as the architect that he was expecting rang the doorbell at that moment, he had to put it to the back of his mind.

It was Monday morning once more and as Lucas went to the village store to perform the daily ritual of buying a morning paper he was relieved to see the red sports car parked outside the surgery.

It had crossed his mind that she might refuse to use it after the way he'd behaved the previous day, but it seemed that either she'd forgiven him or had decided she couldn't manage without it—both reasons enough for him to anticipate a pleasant enough afternoon in the clinic once he'd apologised.

But when he arrived back home his optimism

took a downward plunge. She must have seen him leave the house for those few moments and had pushed a note through the letter box requesting that he remove the car from the surgery forecourt as she would have no further use for it. It was brief and to the point with an underlying message that seemed to say she would have no further use for him either.

He went across immediately, but before doing as she'd asked went inside to see if she was free—a vain hope first thing Monday morning.

It proved to be so. The chairs outside in the corridor were all occupied and all three nurses were busy. Lucy was taking a diabetes clinic, Maria putting a fresh dressing on someone's leg, and Jenna was taking blood for tests that one of the doctors had asked for.

She looked up briefly when he appeared in the doorway and then carried on with what she was doing as if he wasn't there, and on a sudden impulse he went to find Ethan to put before him the decision he'd made during the long hours of the night.

'Hi,' the head of the practice said in a pause between patients, 'What brings you here on a Monday morning when you could be elsewhere?'

'Just a quick question,' Lucas said. 'Would you consider I was letting you down if I went back to working full time at the hospital?'

His friend's eyes widened. 'No, of course not!' he exclaimed. 'It's been great having you around, but you're wasted here, Lucas. As long as you feel you're ready to go back without any qualms, do so by all means. I've heard a few times on the hospital grapevine how much you're missed. And as for being missed, does Jenna know you're planning to get back in harness? She's going to be lost without you around.'

'I'll still be living across the way,' he reminded him, 'and though she doesn't yet know I've made a decision, it was her idea that I go back. I didn't take kindly to the suggestion at the time, but I know she's right. I'm going to contact the hospital trust this morning and set the ball rolling. I should be gone by the end of the week.

'There's just one thing I need to ask of you, Ethan. Would you mind not mentioning it to anyone? I don't want any fuss. I just want to go.'

'You mean you don't even want Jenna to know?'

'I'm not sure at the moment, but I've got all week to think about it, so if you wouldn't mind not saying anything for now.'

'I'm sure she would like to know,' he commented, 'but if that is what you want, I won't say a word.'

'And you'll let me know how things turn out with Francine? I will always make myself available if you need me, Ethan.'

He sighed. 'Thanks for that. She's adamant she wants a divorce and as long as I retain my rights as a father and can see the children whenever I want to, she can have it. There isn't anyone else, as far as I know. Yet I can't believe that she is the woman I married. We're like strangers and I still don't know why she's in such a hurry to throw away what we had.'

* * *

When Lucas went out into the corridor Jenna was passing on her way to Reception with the bloods to go to pathology and he said, 'I'll move the car if you insist, but why make life more difficult when you don't have to?'

'You misunderstand my reason for the request,' she said coolly. 'It is to make life less difficult that I've asked you to move it.'

'As if!' he said tersely, and went to do as she'd asked.

He was sitting down to a late breakfast when the phone rang and a strange voice with an underlying note of urgency in it enquired, 'Is that Dr Devereux?'

'It is,' he replied.

'It's Jack Enderby here,' the voice went on to say. 'Maybe you remember me from Saturday night?'

'Of course I do,' he said immediately. 'How could I forget such a wonderful occasion?'

'It's my dad,' he said. 'I think he's having a heart attack. Can you come out to see him urgently?'

'Of course. I'll be with you in minutes,' he told him, 'but before I set off can you describe his symptoms briefly as I may need to ring for an ambulance straight away rather than waiting until I arrive at the farm? If it is a heart attack then every minute is precious.'

'Agonising chest pains, short of breath, cold and clammy, and he's blue around the lips.'

'I'll phone for an ambulance now and then be on my way. Keep him warm and don't leave his side for a moment until I get there.'

Lucas was getting into his car even as he was speaking and dialling the emergency services at the same time, then he rang Ethan on his private number and said briefly, 'Can you spare Jenna for a while? There's an emergency at Wheatlands Farm.

'George Enderby is having what sounds like a massive heart attack and I might need some assistance until the emergency services arrive. Tell her that the red car is on my drive and the keys are in the ignition.'

'Right,' he said. 'She'll be with you as fast as she can. Poor old George.'

As Lucas drove the short distance to the farm he could see the red car bobbing along some distance behind him and thought that Jenna wouldn't be pleased to be back in the sports car after making the gesture of handing it back to him, but she would be most upset to hear about George, and if there was anyone who got their priorities right, she did.

When he pulled up outside the farmhouse she screeched to a stop behind him and as they flung themselves out of the cars Jack Enderby came running out of the house white-faced and shaking.

'It's too late!' he cried. 'He's gone. Dad isn't breathing.'

As they ran past him Lucas said, 'Where is he?'

'On the floor in the lounge. I was afraid to move him.'

In seconds Lucas was crouched beside the still figure, testing for a heartbeat, while Jenna crouched on the other side. She was pale but calm and Lucas said urgently, 'He hasn't left us yet. There is a faint heartbeat. I'll take the mouth while you do the chest compressions.' They began the desperate process of resuscitation, with Lucas pinching the old man's nose and breathing into his mouth once to each of her five compressions.

After what seemed like for ever he exclaimed, 'He's back with us, Jenna. See his chest starting to rise and fall. Keep up the good work, the ambulance shouldn't be long.'

'I don't believe it!' their host of Saturday night gasped as they continued with the treatment. 'I was sure we'd lost him.'

'Your father isn't out of danger yet,' Lucas told him. 'He's on medication that I've prescribed. Has he been taking it regularly?'

'As far as I know,' was the answer, 'but we've been so busy with the harvest I must confess that I haven't been taking note. If he comes out of this I'll monitor his drug intake more carefully.'

The ambulance had arrived. They could hear it screeching to a halt outside, followed by the sound of running feet, and Jenna let out a sigh of relief.

This was the last thing she'd been expecting—being back with Lucas, doing the job they were trained for, and having to eat humble pie by using his car again. Returning it had backfired on her.

'Thanks for that,' Lucas said evenly to her when the ambulance had gone, with its siren breaking into the autumn morning and Jack sitting protectively in the back beside his father as a paramedic gave George oxygen. 'It made all the difference, having you there.'

'I have my uses sometimes,' she said coolly, 'and Lucy would have been just as capable.'

'Hardly! Lucy is a gem, but she hasn't been helping in my clinic and hasn't worked in a coronary unit, as you have. You'll have to tell me where it was one day. I somehow have a feeling that it wasn't on this side of the Channel.'

'Does it matter where it was?' she said quietly. She got behind the wheel of the red car once more. 'I'll leave this where I found it.' And before he could protest she was away.

* * *

The only good thing about the manner of their parting at Wheatlands Farm as far as Lucas was concerned was the knowledge that Jenna would be helping him in the clinic that afternoon. It would be a chance to talk to her, to apologise for his heated words yesterday.

He wanted to tell her that he was going back to the hospital but felt he had to find the right moment, and had to get used to the idea first. Going back there had become an issue instead of part of the natural way of things, and his outburst when she'd suggested it was not going to make the telling any easier…

To his dismay it was Lucy who came to assist him at the clinic that afternoon and when he asked what had happened to Jenna she said, 'I know I'm a poor replacement, but Jenna was knocked off her bicycle when she was cycling back here after lunch.'

'What?' he exclaimed. 'Is she badly hurt?'

'No, just cuts and bruises, but Ethan has told her to take the afternoon off, and knowing her she's probably gone down to the beach as salt water is a great healer.'

'Yes, it is,' he agreed soberly, but it wouldn't heal the breach that he'd caused between them, would it? As soon as his clinic was over he would go to check how badly she'd been hurt. He needed to see that she was all right. No doubt he would be as welcome as a wet day for a wedding, but he was still going to call at Four Winds House before he called it a day.

It proved not to be as easy as he'd imagined it. There were more patients than usual at the clinic and it didn't go as smoothly with Lucy's help as it did with Jenna's, so by the time he was driving down the hill towards the headland it was early evening.

When he got there, just as yesterday, there was no family car on the drive, just Jenna's bicycle looking somewhat the worse for wear with bent mudguards and twisted handlebars. When he rang the doorbell and got no reply he decided he would spend the time sorting the bike out until she put in an appearance—he always carried a tool kit in the boot of his car.

The easiest thing would be to suggest she use the sports car again, but he had a pretty good idea what she would say to that. So he stuck to plan A and repaired the bicycle. It would need one or two spare parts and wouldn't be safe to ride until they were in place, but once that was done it would be roadworthy once more.

But where was she? he wondered as he propped the bike up against the garden fence and pinned a note on it to explain what he'd done and that it wasn't yet safe to ride.

He'd been down to the beach and there'd been no sight of her. She wasn't at home, so where was she—the hospital? He hoped not, but could soon find out.

At that moment she appeared, moving slowly along the headland towards the house, and when she saw him her step faltered.

She looked dejected, was limping, and he waited to see what she would do when she drew level.

'I'm sorry about this afternoon,' she said before he had the chance to speak. 'I didn't want to let you down but when Ethan heard that the dog from the post office had come dashing out and knocked me off my bicycle he insisted that I take the afternoon off, and I thought you might feel that having to manage on your own was the lesser of two evils.'

'Lucy helped me,' he said levelly. 'What's the matter with your foot?'

'Nothing serious. I twisted my ankle when I fell off the bike.'

'So let's go inside and I'll take a look at it.'

'I am a nurse,' she protested. 'I would know if I'd fractured a bone or pulled a ligament.'

'Nevertheless, I want to make sure, so can we go in?'

'If you insist,' she said, unlocking the door.

'I take it that your parents are out.'

'Yes, Mum had a hospital appointment at the coronary clinic and Dad said he would see what he could find out regarding George while they were there.'

'And you didn't go with them to have your foot X-rayed?'

'No. It happened after they'd gone.'

He followed her inside and they both sat down in the living room.

'So take your shoe off,' he said, expecting her to protest at the fuss, but she didn't and when he saw how swollen and bruised her foot was he understood why.

Taking it between his hands, he felt it gently and she melted at his touch. How could she be angry with this wonderful man? she thought weakly, gazing down at hair as dark as ebony and the tanned stem of his neck as he bent over her foot.

He looked up and caught her glance on him but didn't respond in any way and Jenna thought, he hasn't forgotten the quarrel. Lucas still thinks I'm an interfering nuisance. Wincing at the effort, she withdrew her foot out of his clasp.

'I'm taking you to A and E,' he informed her, ignoring the gesture. 'I don't think there is a fracture or you wouldn't have been walking on it the way you were, but you're a nurse, for goodness' sake, Jenna. You should have had it checked over.'

She managed a smile but it was an effort. 'Aren't those in the medical profession known to be slow to treat themselves?'

She saw amusement in the dark hazel eyes observing her and wondered if she would ever understand this man who held her heart in his capable hands.

When she got to her feet he said, 'You've been on them long enough without an X-ray,' and picked her up into his arms and carried her out to the car.

He was silent as he pointed the Mercedes in the direction of the major road that led to the hospital and she said, 'I haven't asked how the clinic was today. Were there many there?'

In spite of their differences she was upset to have missed it, but it sounded as if she was making conversation and he replied briefly, 'It went well and, yes, there were a lot of patients.'

His mind was on where they were going and if anyone yet knew that he was returning to the fold on the coming Monday. It would be typical of the way things were going for the two of them if Jenna found out from another source.

He wanted to tell her himself and if it didn't make her see how much respect and regard for her he had and how important she was in his life, he didn't know what would.

He almost told her then but felt it wasn't the right moment in the circumstances, and the fact that they wouldn't be going anywhere near the coronary unit made it seem safe to take the risk, but when the hospital gates loomed up ahead, instead of parking on the staff spot that was still his he used one of the places available to the public, and told her to stay there while he went to find a wheelchair.

Her foot had been X-rayed and there were no fractures, which, considering the number of bones present in that part of the body, was surprising.

There'd been a couple of young registrars nearby while he'd been waiting for her to come out of Radiology and one of them said in a voice he mistakenly thought wouldn't be overheard,

'That was bossy Balfour's daughter. Half of the unattached guys in this place have tried to date her at one time or another but all they ever got was a big smile and a "no, thank you".'

'So who's the guy with her?' his companion asked.

'Looks familiar, but can't place him,' was the reply.

As Lucas turned away to hide a smile Jenna reappeared with the news that there were no fractures, and, deciding that any other treatment such as cold compresses or applications of witch hazel she could do herself, they returned to the car in the autumn dusk.

He was smiling as the car pulled out of the hospital car park and she observed him questioningly.

'I'm thinking of a conversation I heard while you were being X-rayed,' he explained.

'What about?'

'You.'

'Me?'

'A couple of young registrars were discussing your popularity with the male staff of Hunters Hill. How you always said no when asked for a date.'

'Oh, that! It would be when I was home on vacation from college. I used to work on the wards as a trainee for experience and extra cash. *Did they recognise you?*'

'Er, no,' he said whimsically, 'but one of them thought I seemed familiar. They had no problem deciding who you were, but I was a nonentity.'

As she joined in his laughter at that, Jenna was happy, happy that they were back on the same wavelength, that her foot wasn't fractured, and that life was going to be as wonderful as it had been before, with Lucas running his heart clinic and living in The Old Chart House close by. Maybe one day he would feel he could go back to the hospital and then she would know for certain that his demons had gone.

Thinking back to what he'd overheard, she thought what a randy lot those young doctors at the hospital had been. There'd been some sort of competition amongst them to get her into bed, but it hadn't worked. And now, when she was ready to give heart, body and soul to the man beside her, he wasn't taking her up on the offer.

'I repaired your bike while I was waiting for you to show up,' he said, breaking into her thoughts.

When she observed him in amazement, he said, 'No need to look so surprised—putting things back together again is part of my job. It still needs a couple of small parts to be replaced, which I'll get tomorrow, and when I've done that you'll be able to ride it again. The next time I call in at the post office I will be telling the guy who owns it to keep his animal on a leash. Tell me, what was so important that you went walking on an injured foot?'

What indeed? she thought. Themselves, of course. She'd come home to help care for her mother and had met a very special man that she knew she was going to love for the rest of her life.

But had she been taking too much for granted? He was way above her, high up in the medical world with no ties to bind him, and didn't want her in his bed. Those were the kinds of concerns that had sent her out walking on a badly bruised foot.

CHAPTER EIGHT

KEITH and Barbara had arrived back long before them and the moment her mother saw that Jenna was limping she was the doctor once more and wanted to know what was wrong.

'The big collie from the post office came gambolling out as I was going past on my bicycle and knocked me off,' she told her. 'I hurt my foot when I fell and as it was swollen and bruised Lucas took me to A and E to have it X-rayed.'

'And what was the result?'

'No fractures, just swelling,' she told her. 'And what about you? What did they have to say on the coronary unit?'

Here we go, Lucas thought. The moment of truth had arrived. But Barbara merely said,

'My heart isn't good, but the angioplasty seems to be working and they were reasonably optimistic that I might be around a little longer to plague you than I'd at first thought, due entirely to you being there when I needed you, Lucas.'

'It's what I've been trained for, Dr Balfour,' he reminded her, 'and every time I put that training into practice there is a great feeling of usefulness.'

He was smiling and there was relief in it. It would seem that the news of his return hadn't yet filtered through. There were four days left for him to tell Jenna and then he would be gone, but only from the practice. He would still be living in Bluebell Cove. Nothing on earth was going to make him move out of The Old Chart House, unless at some time in the future she didn't want to live there with him.

It was her father's turn to contribute to the conversation and he said, 'We saw George Enderby while we were there and, considering that he almost died, the old fellow is holding onto life very well. There was some talk of surgery that I didn't quite grasp, but you'll understand that more than I do, Lucas.'

'Jack and his wife were with him and said to tell you both how grateful all the family are for what you did for George. If you hadn't been there they would have lost him, that's for sure.'

For the rest of the week Lucas kept a low profile until Thursday afternoon came along and with it his last clinic. This time Jenna was there as he saw each patient, her swollen foot having responded to treatment, and totally unaware that it was the last time they would be together as doctor and nurse.

After taking her to A and E on Monday he'd avoided contact, wanting to tell her that he was doing as she'd suggested and yet holding back. Supposing his fears and uncertainties came back and he found he'd made a mistake? he kept thinking. How would she feel then, knowing that it was at her insistence that he'd moved back to Hunters Hill?

He was going. Wasn't going to change his

mind on that. He'd always been a man of his word, afraid of nothing until the motiveless attack that had scarred him for ever. Would it be better if she were to find out when he'd actually made the move and was more confident that it had been the right thing to do? he pondered. Because he would soon know if it was.

When the last patient had gone and there was just the two of them, he was besieged by an aching feeling of farewell, even though he would only be working a couple of miles away and would be back in the village for all the rest of the time. But she wouldn't be part of his working life any more and he was going to regret that.

Always quick to tune in to his moods she asked, 'What's wrong? Why so glum?'

'It was just a thought that came into my mind, and now it's gone.'

'And are you going to tell me what it was?'

'Probably, but not now. Some time over the weekend maybe.'

'Why not now?'

Because then will be my last chance, he thought. I've been getting myself psyched up all week to tell you that we won't be working together any more, that I'm doing what you suggested and hoping that it's the right thing.

He didn't reply.

'Are you ill?' she persisted.

'No.'

'You're worried about Ethan?'

'No, none of those things, so let it pass, will you, please, Jenna?'

'You won't let me into your life, will you?' she said evenly. 'You'd be a wow in M15. Whereas *my life is an open book as far as you're concerned.*'

'Yes, I know,' he agreed patiently, 'but you have been fortunate to have escaped life's hurts so far. You're uncomplicated and serene, like the still waters of a lake, rather than the surging sea, and I don't want to be responsible for taking that away from you by making any wrong moves.'

'You make it sound as if our lives are a board

game!' she cried, 'and don't forget I've had my share of bad times with a mother who fitted me in when she had a moment to spare, though I was fortunate that Dad was always there for me, kind and loving, making it all bearable.

'One thing is for sure, when I have children they won't ever be kept on the edge of my life. They will be adored as much as I adore their father, whoever he might be.'

She was about to go back to the nurses' room, having said her piece, and he asked, 'So am I still in the running for that role? Or have you given up on me?'

As if, she thought. How could she ever give up on him? But because she was smarting she couldn't resist pointing to the ringless third finger of her left hand and telling him before she went, 'Watch this space.'

If he hadn't been feeling so down at the thought of not being in her working life any more he might have laughed at the threat and taken her in his arms, but the space on her finger wasn't the only space he was aware of.

There was the one beside him in the big double bed where he slept alone, and whose fault was that? Not hers. He'd refused her because of his pride, and because she was beautiful and generous, and deserved better than some guy who'd made a huge error of judgement.

So where did they go from here? She'd been pointing out the lack of a ring to get back at him because he was keeping her on the surface of things again, but the conversation he'd overheard at the hospital between the two young doctors had been like a warning.

Jenna wasn't going to want to wait for ever while he blew hot and cold as she saw it. There were plenty of other fish in Bluebell Cove, *in and out of the sea.*

Once he had made the huge step back to reality at Hunters Hill he would ask her to marry him, and if she said yes it would be like the dawn after a long night because he couldn't deny that he loved her any longer.

But before that he had to tell her what he was going to do. That today had been his last clinic, his last connection with the practice, but hopefully it wouldn't be his last connection with her.

He went round to Four Winds House on Sunday morning, aware that he'd left the telling of his plans a bit late, but at least he was here, he thought as he scanned the beach for any sign of her.

She wasn't there and there were no signs of life at the house. As he stood on the drive, non-plussed, Lucy came along, walking her dog. When she saw him she called, 'They've gone to relatives in Yorkshire for the weekend, all three of them, and won't be back until early Monday morning. I imagine Jenna will go straight to the surgery.'

He'd blown it, he thought wretchedly. By the time she came back the first day of his return to the hospital would already be under way.

'Do you know where?' he asked.

She shook her head. 'No, I'm sorry, I don't, Dr Devereux.'

* * *

The weekend seemed endless. She couldn't wait for Monday to come, with the heart clinic in the afternoon, Jenna kept thinking. It had been a spur-of-the-moment decision to join her parents for a short break and she was regretting it.

Barbara and Keith had arranged to stay with his sister and her husband in the Yorkshire Dales, and her aunt and uncle had been keen for her to go with them, not having seen her since she'd come back from abroad.

She was on a low after losing her temper at the end of the heart clinic and had agreed to accompany them as she was feeling that every time she was with Lucas, something went wrong. Now, however, she couldn't wait for the weekend to be over.

After an early start her father dropped her off at the surgery on Monday morning. Her spirits were lifting because she would soon see Lucas again. There was no sign of him at his house but she didn't see anything strange in that and hurried inside to get the day under way.

The morning brought into the surgery a case of shingles: the chickenpox virus, sometimes having lain dormant in the body for years and then flaring up again in a nasty and sometimes serious form.

It was Jacintha, who was in charge of the Tourist Information Office down on the coast road, and when Ethan saw the half-circle of angry red blisters starting in the middle of her chest and ending between her shoulder blades, he said sympathetically, 'It's shingles, Jacintha, that's the bad news. The good news is that you haven't got it in your eyes, on your scalp or various other parts of the body where it would be so much harder to cope with. How long is it since the blisters appeared?'

'Only this morning,' she informed him. 'I've never seen shingles before, but the pain was so severe and so strange that I did wonder.'

He nodded. 'You're right about the discomfort. But these days we can do something about it, if not remove it completely. There are anti-viral medications that if taken very early in the illness will make the recovery period much less agonising.'

'Will I have to stay off work?' she asked anxiously.

'Yes, I think you should. You are likely to feel very tired while taking the antiviral drugs and for a week or two afterwards. There is also a risk that anyone who has not had chickenpox could contract it if they were in direct contact. That could have particular repercussions if they were pregnant. Stay home and take it easy for a while.'

'I will,' she said fervently, and departed with a prescription for the antiviral tablets in her hand.

When she'd gone Ethan said to the nurses, 'It will be interesting to see if any more cases of shingles appear, or if an epidemic of chickenpox is about to descend on us.'

He glanced across at Jenna, who was doing a diabetic blood test on a patient, and said, 'There won't be a heart clinic this afternoon, Jenna, so you won't need to come back after lunch.'

'Right,' she said, her eyes widening, and left

it at that, but as soon as she was free she went to have a word with him.

'Is Lucas all right?' she asked.

'Yes, he's fine,' he assured her, and felt like throttling his friend for letting him in for what was coming next.

'So why—?'

'Is there no clinic, were you going to say?'

'Yes.'

'Lucas has gone back to the hospital to take up where he left off,' he said uncomfortably, and unwittingly added to her dismay. 'I think he feels that there is nothing further for him here and he's probably right. A village practice isn't the place for a surgeon of his repute. His skills and expertise will be put to much better use in a large hospital.'

'Yes, of course,' she said slowly, as if her thinking processes had run out of steam. 'Thanks for explaining, Ethan.'

'So are you all right with that?' he asked gently.

'Yes, I'm fine. He's made the right decision. I wish him well.'

'He'll be back here in Bluebell Cove tonight,' he reminded her. 'He hasn't gone to the moon.'

'No, of course not,' she said in the same stilted kind of voice, and went back to her duties.

For the rest of the morning she presented a calm exterior that gave no inkling of the confusion beneath, but when it was lunchtime she couldn't wait to get away to sort out her thoughts.

Lucas going back to Hunters Hill without telling her was another instance of him keeping her on the sidelines of his life, she thought miserably. It had been her suggestion that he go back to his own domain and he'd snapped at her, why, she still wasn't sure, but he had, and then, lo and behold, without so much as a word he'd done what she'd suggested.

It had been clear from the way Ethan had answered her questions that he felt sorry for her and the thought of being an object of pity was bringing a flush to her cheeks.

Loving Lucas was just too complicated, she thought miserably. The next time they met she

219

was going to tell him he could stop worrying, she'd given up on him, much though it would break her heart to do it.

He'd been welcomed back to Hunters Hill Hospital with smiles all round by the staff of the coronary unit. They'd even produced champagne to celebrate the occasion and Lucas knew he ought to be content. He was up to a point, but he wished that Jenna was there. It was she who had inspired him to come back and he hoped that when he next saw her she would be happy for him.

He'd got out of the habit of working late while he'd been part of The Tides practice, but it was nine o'clock when he arrived home that evening. The first thing he did was phone the house on the headland, only to be told by Keith that Jenna wasn't there and she hadn't left any message for him.

She was where he'd thought she would be, a solitary figure on the beach, visible only by the light of an autumn moon, and he knew instinctively that he'd made a mess of things just when he wanted everything to be all right.

He called her name as he walked across the wet sand, not wanting to startle her, and she turned slowly.

'It was my first day back and I had a late finish,' he said softly. 'I take it that Ethan explained?'

'Oh, yes, he explained,' she said flatly. 'Explained that you'd left the practice and gone back to where you belong.'

'Hey! Just a moment!' he protested. 'I've done what you wanted me to do. Aren't you pleased?'

'Of course I am! How could I not be? But Ethan having to tell me did rather take the edge off it, even though I accepted that it was just further proof that you only want me on the edge of your life, and you can have that. Lucas, from now on I'll stay where you want me to stay, at a distance.'

As he stepped forward to take her in his arms and explain what his motives had been she said, 'Don't touch me!' And without a backward glance she pointed herself in the direction of the twinkling lights of the house she called home, leaving him to gaze bleakly out to sea.

* * *

As October bowed out and November took over, the chill of winter descended on Bluebell Cove. The first fall of snow came crisp and early on a very cold day, but Jenna hardly noticed it. Her heart had been wrapped around with ice ever since that night on the beach.

She knew deep down that she'd made too big a thing about Lucas not telling her he was going back to work in the hospital, but it had just been one occasion too many of him keeping her on hold, and it had been too much.

What was it with him? she asked herself a thousand times. Was it still a case of once bitten twice shy after his experience with Philippa? Surely not. By nature he was cool and confident, not usually easily rattled, so it must be something about herself that still made him wary of any kind of commitment.

He probably had her catalogued as too eager, too anxious to have his ring on her finger, when in truth all she wanted from him was tenderness, and there was no sign of that. Since those last moments on the beach they'd only seen each other rarely.

When they had he'd been polite but distant and she'd tried to console herself with the thought that it was less painful that way, then had gone home and wept.

He worked late most nights and she would sit hunched on the window seat in her bedroom, watching for the Mercedes coming along the coast road, wishing that she had the right to be waiting for him with a glowing log fire and a nourishing meal, instead of having to make do with caring about him from a distance.

On the evening of the day that the snow had been floating down in white perfection, instead of keeping her vigil on the bedroom window seat, Jenna was about to make her way home from the community centre where the children from the village school, who prided themselves on their brass band, had been giving a concert.

As she began to walk through the village it was a magical sight with the lights from the windows of the houses shining out across the snow, until she came to The Old Chart House standing dark and forlorn because its owner wasn't yet home from the day's toil, and she thought that the red sports car didn't look much happier standing unloved and unused on the drive beneath a covering of snow.

On impulse she went next door to Ethan's house and when he saw her standing on the step he exclaimed, 'Jenna! What's wrong? It isn't often *you* come knocking on my door.'

'Yes, I know,' she agreed quickly, 'but I've just noticed that Lucas isn't home yet.'

'That isn't surprising. Operating theatres are known to be busy places. There isn't much we can do about that, I'm afraid.'

'Do you have a key?'

'Er, yes, but why?'

'I thought I'd go in, put some lights on and get the fire going so that it doesn't look so cheerless when he arrives.'

'The central heating will be on,' he pointed out.

'Yes, I know, but there's nothing cheerful about a radiator, is there?'

'No, I suppose not. You can have the key, no trouble. Lucas is short of some tender loving care.' He gave a wry smile. 'Aren't we all?'

He turned towards the hall table and, picking up the key lying there, said, 'Here, take it, and if you have time to put some food in the oven I'm sure it would be appreciated as he never seems to have time to eat these days.'

When he'd closed the door and gone back to ironing his shirts, he was smiling. If he wasn't able to sort out his own affairs of the heart, at least he could put in a good word for his friend.

Once inside Jenna moved with speed. Within seconds the lights were on, the fire glowing, and a 'cook from frozen' meat dish was in the oven. On the point of making a quick departure and dropping the key through Ethan's letter box, she heard his car pull up outside and groaned. She'd been quick, but not quick enough.

He was in like a flash, at the worst expecting a break-in. When he found her standing motionless in the kitchen he exclaimed, 'Jenna! What are *you* doing here?'

'I was passing, saw the house was in darkness and thought it would seem rather cheerless when you got in, so I borrowed your key from Ethan and came in to switch on the lights and create a more welcoming atmosphere. The snow is very early this year and, beautiful as it is, it brings a chill with it.'

She was gabbling and knew it. He hadn't been able to get a word in edgeways since his amazed greeting when he'd found her there, and she hadn't finished yet. 'I took the liberty of looking in the freezer and found a ready meal, which is in the oven and shouldn't be long.'

He made no comment about that, just nodded and said, 'What are you doing up here in the village without transport? Is your bicycle still not usable?'

'No, it's fine, but I didn't come out on it tonight as there is snow around. I've been to a brass band concert at the community centre given by the village schoolchildren.'

'Really,' he said absently.

'Yes, really, and now I'm going as I'm sure you must be ready to unwind in front of the fire.'

'There's no need to rush off if you don't have to,' he said quickly. He could have told her that he'd already eaten, but that would take the edge off her thoughtfulness, and if she was still here when the food was cooked, he would force it down if it choked him.

She was standing irresolute, wanting to stay so much she could taste it, but aware that she'd intruded into his life again. Her being there hadn't been at his request so there was nothing to get all dreamy about.

'How are you?' he asked, breaking into her thoughts. 'Are you happy, Jenna?'

'I'm all right, I suppose. What about you?'

'I'm the same. I've settled back into the old routine better than I expected. It's very busy, which is why I'm working such long hours, but it gets the days over as well as helping to keep people healthy. Ethan keeps me informed about the practice. He says that Leo has fitted in a treat, and that Lucy keeps promising to retire.'

'And what does he say about me?'

That your light has gone out would be the truth, he thought, but he couldn't tell her that. The words would stick in his throat, knowing that he was to blame, so he said, 'Only good things, Jenna.' He made a swift change of subject. 'When the food is cooked I'll either walk you home or take you in the car, which-ever you prefer.'

'Yes, but you must eat first,' she insisted.

'All right, but I won't sleep easy unless I know you're safe and that you've not done any detours in the direction of sand and sea.'

He hadn't slept easily any night since those awful moments on the beach that had ended in her telling him not to touch her. It had been that which had made him decide to let Jenna get on with her life without him in it, and it had taken every ounce of willpower he possessed to stick to that decision. But now here she was, caught in the act of trying to look after him, and all his resolves were crumbling.

The table was set and she was taking the food out of the oven. When she'd put it in front of him she went into the sitting room and kept out of sight until he'd finished eating, but the moment he went into the kitchen with the empty plate, grateful that she hadn't been there to witness the effort he'd made to get the food down, she was there, ready to set off home.

But not in the car, it would seem, as she was saying, 'Thanks for the offer to see me home, but I'd like to walk if you don't mind. The snow is clean and crisp, having only recently fallen, and I love to walk on it when it's like that.'

She'd come up with a reason not to be in the car with him on the spur of the moment because they would be in too close proximity. The sight of his hands on the steering-wheel with those supple surgeon's fingers, the dark hazel eyes observing her that could make her wilt at a glance and the tantalising male smell of him would have her weak and wanting before she was halfway there, and what would it achieve? Just more pain and misery when he drove off and left her at Four Winds House.

'OK,' he said blandly, as if he hadn't tuned in to why she didn't want to go home in the car. He wanted her to stay, he wanted to carry her up to his bedroom and make love to her, but he accepted that short of handcuffing her to the furniture there was no way he could keep her there any longer. So it was going to be a walk in the snow and he wondered what Jenna would think if she knew what had been going through his mind.

There was a keen frost outside. The softness of the snow had become icy and when he took her hand in his to prevent her from slipping, Jenna observed him sombrely.

'I wasn't intending to be there when you came home,' she said as if she'd been caught out in a crime. 'Another few seconds and I would have gone.'

'And you weren't going to leave a note?' he exclaimed in mock dismay. 'How would I have known who the kind fairy was?'

She was smiling now. 'You would have known because Ethan would have told you.'

It was his turn to be serious now. 'What made you do it? We haven't seen each other for weeks and then out of the blue you appear in my life again.'

'Yours was the only house in darkness, which meant you were working late. I just wanted to brighten it up for when you came home, that was all.'

It was another half-truth. She *had* wanted it to look more welcoming but it wasn't just that. It was because she still loved him so much, wanted to be there to care for him, but she was being denied the opportunity because of a situation that they were equally responsible for.

From his manner it seemed as if Lucas was reasonably pleased to see her but not exactly jumping for joy, and there was no way she wanted to open up old hurts by leaving herself so vulnerable again.

So when they reached the headland she gently disengaged her hand from his and said quickly, 'Thank you for walking me home,

Lucas.' As he opened his mouth to speak she was gone, moving swiftly up the driveway.

He'd been going to ask her out to dinner to celebrate what might be a new beginning but Jenna had been too quick for him. She'd gone before he could make the suggestion.

As he turned to trudge back the way they'd come there was the determination inside him not to be put off, and if she thought that she'd just slotted him into his place in her life even more firmly than before, she was mistaken.

Finding her rooted to the spot in his kitchen had been like the sun coming from behind a cloud. For a moment it felt like his broken heart had been cured. He should have known better than to expect it to be so simple,

'Don't touch me!' she'd cried all those barren weeks ago. He had yet to find out if she still felt the same way in spite of her solicitude on his behalf.

When Jenna saw Ethan the next morning he said, 'So how did it go?'

She smiled. 'As well as could be expected, to quote an often-used medical description. Did Lucas say anything to you about catching me on the premises?'

'When he brought the key back he said that it had been a surprise.'

'That was it! Nothing else?'

'There was one other thing, but I don't think you'll want to hear it.'

'Nevertheless, tell me what it was,' she persisted.

'It was that he'd stopped off for a meal on the way home and had already eaten.'

'Oh, no!' she groaned. 'So he wouldn't have been hungry?'

'Not very, I imagine, but in light of your concern for him he wasn't going to spoil it, was he? So he ate the spaghetti bolognese like a true son of Devon,' he concluded laughingly, and she couldn't help but join in.

Maybe she should slip a card advertising the local slimming club under his door, she thought, but deep down she was mortified at the way she'd taken his eating arrangements for granted.

It was no use fretting, though. The incident was over, dead and gone. She'd thought that Lucas might follow her when she'd gone flouncing off into the house the night before, but it had been a vain hope, and now it was just another day at The Tides, starting with Eddie from the post office appearing with a gash in his leg that he should have gone straight to A and E with as there was blood everywhere.

'I was cutting a stone block with an electric saw and the blade slipped and sliced into my leg,' he said calmly, and promptly fainted as she tried to stem the blood. Lucy was assisting, an ambulance was already on its way, and the feeling that it was just another day at the surgery was disappearing fast.

Unaware that the heart clinic and the man in charge of it had gone, a patient had been brought to the surgery by his wife with severe pains on one side of his chest, and as he had a history of heart problems they'd thought they were doing the sensible thing by taking a short cut to see a top heart surgeon in Bluebell Cove.

'I'm afraid that Dr Devereux has gone back to Hunters Hill Hospital,' Ethan told them as the patient collapsed on to the nearest chair. Calling for Jenna to join him while he examined the man, he asked the wife to unbutton her husband's shirt, and doctor and nurse stared in surprise at the sight of the tell-tale signs of shingles again.

'How long have you had shingles?' Ethan asked, pointing to the bright red blisters arrayed across the left side of his chest like a scattering of oddly shaped rubies.

'What? Oh, about a week,' was the answer.

'And have you already had chickenpox?' he questioned, and the man nodded. 'So the pain might be coming from the shingles.'

'I've had no pain from them so far,' he protested.

'That is odd,' Ethan commented. 'Pain is the name of the game with shingles, and you haven't got the usual signs of heart failure, such as shortage of breath, sweating and blueness of the face.'

'I know!' he groaned, 'but the pain is in the same place as when I had the heart attack.'

'Then I think you should go to the hospital anyway and get fully checked out,' said Ethan, and called for an ambulance.

When they'd gone with the sirens of a second ambulance breaking into the silence of the village that morning, Jenna said, 'That's the second shingles case and they aren't connected in any way. What do you think is going on?'

'I don't know,' he replied. 'The antiviral tablets take away some of the pain, but not all of it, by any means. I'm wondering if that fellow is getting an accumulation of the shingles pain because he hasn't had any so far. We'll have to wait until we get the report from the hospital and, with Hunters Hill in mind, Jack Enderby rang last night to say that George is home and singing the praises of yourself and another miracle worker who shall be nameless.'

When the morning was over and she'd cycled home, her father met her at the door and said,

'A bouquet of flowers has arrived for you, Jenna. They're in your room. Can I make a guess who they're from?'

She was already halfway up the stairs, but stopped and went back down to where he was smiling up at her. Kissing him on his weathered cheek, she said, 'There is only one person I want them to be from, Dad. Keep your fingers crossed for me.'

'Lucas Devereux?'

'Yes, who else?'

'You know that your mother is very taken with him, don't you, which is a major step towards peace in our time. A top surgeon and charismatic with it. What more could she ask for in a son-in-law?'

'Someone who really loves me, maybe?'

He didn't delve into the complexities of that, just gave her a gentle push and said, 'So go and see who your flowers are from.'

They *were* from Lucas, long-stemmed cream and yellow roses and blue irises. As she picked up the card that was with them, the words on it, written in a bold hand, said briefly, 'Thank you for last night. It was a lovely thought.'

One step forward, she thought achingly as she sank down onto the bed with them in her arms, and hoped that Lucas wasn't suffering from chronic indigestion due to his overeating of the previous night.

CHAPTER NINE

THE snow had been and gone in a couple of days, so swiftly, so soon, it was hard to believe it had actually fallen, but it had and with it had come the reminder that Christmas was coming, not yet, but soon enough for the festivities committee to start making preparations for what were to be the two highlights of the season in Bluebell Cove.

It was the combination of coast and countryside that made Jenna love the place so much, and this time it had been decided that as well as having a big Christmas tree in the centre of the village, there should also be another on the headland overlooking the sea, and that on Christmas Eve the villagers would dress up in their finest, take a partner, and dance from one to the other with music laid on, followed by a buffet at the community centre.

Before that, in mid-December, there was to be a nativity play, performed on the beach between tides instead of in the old Norman church that stood in the centre of the village.

Both ideas had been welcomed wholeheartedly because of their special appeal, and along with other regular festivities being planned, the village was gradually getting organised for the season.

In the normal way of things Jenna would have been at the heart of the preparations, but this time Christmas loomed as an ordeal to be got through.

Not so for Meredith from the Mariner's Mooring guest house. They were already fully booked for Christmas and New Year, and she seemed to have the polymyalgia well under control each time she came for an ESR blood test, so at least someone was happy.

Jenna hadn't spoken to Lucas after receiving the bouquet but had sent him a brief thank-you note and waited for what was coming next...if anything.

In the meantime, the days dragged by slowly. Until Friday lunchtime when she came out of the surgery to go home and found him leaning against the wall that separated the practice from the road.

'Would you be free to go for a meal this evening?' he said without wasting words. 'It's the first night I've had off since we last met and I wouldn't be here now if two big operations hadn't been postponed. So what do you say, Jenna?'

'I say do you still stop off for something to eat on your way home?'

He observed her questioningly for a moment and then said between a laugh and a groan, 'I know who told you that. Wait until I see Ethan! Yes, I have been doing that, but it didn't stop me from enjoying the spaghetti bolognese. But I won't be eating tonight, in the hope that you will let me wine and dine you. Will you?' he asked her again.

'Yes. I would like that, *as a friend*. What time must I be ready?'

He'd got the message. It said don't mess with

my feelings, but he gave no sign and said equally, 'I realise that you'll want to see your mother settled for the night first, so maybe you should suggest a time.'

'Is half past eight all right?'

'Of course. Do you want to go in the Red Peril or the Mercedes?'

'I don't mind, it's up to you. Where will we be going, exactly?'

'There's a hotel further along the coast that serves good food and has fantastic views from the dining room in daylight, which of course will be well gone by the time we arrive. But tonight there will be a full moon so we might still be able to soak up some of the atmosphere. It's just the sort of place *for friends to meet*,' he said with gentle mockery.

'You seem to know,' she parried. 'How many times have you been there?'

'None. I've always lacked the impetus before, though I've heard excellent reports of it.' Then, his tone becoming more brisk, he went on, 'But you were about to go home for lunch and I'm taking up your time, so eight-thirty it is, Jenna. I'll see you then.'

As she cycled home she was wishing she hadn't made the jibe about being just friends. She wanted them to be lovers before all else, and friends because they were lovers, not the other way round. Nevertheless, she'd meant the comment as a reminder to Lucas that she was still intending that he should have a lesser role in her life.

That kind of reasoning lasted until he came to pick her up dressed in well-cut tweeds with a shirt that most men would die for, and with hand-made shoes on his feet.

He had dressed up for her, she thought as her heartbeat quickened, but, then, he would. Lucas Devereux never did things by halves and that brought her down to earth. It was the reason why she was living in limbo, the reason why he wasn't going to commit himself to the blonde that he'd first seen flirting with the lifeguard. The easy-peasy one who wasn't fussy who she slept with.

Yet he knew from the conversation he'd heard between the two doctors that day at the hospital that she didn't sleep around.

And now he was holding the car door open for her to get in and tuning into her lack of enthusiasm at the same time. Yet she was dressed in the colours he loved to see her in, cream, gold and blue, the colours of the flowers in the bouquet he'd sent her, so maybe he was mistaking her mood.

She was wearing a long cream skirt with a pale yellow top and a bright blue linen jacket and as she settled into the passenger seat of the Mercedes Jenna was smiling, her darker thoughts put to one side in the pleasure of being with him once again.

Tonight their closeness in the car was not going to be a barrier, she'd decided. When she'd told him she preferred to walk that other time after her impulsive and clumsy attempt to bring him some cheer on a cold winter night it had been different.

On both occasions they hadn't seen each other

for weeks but this time it hadn't been a case of her sneaking into his house without being invited. He'd been waiting outside the surgery to extend the invitation on the first day he was free and had made it clear that he wanted her to say yes.

As the car moved smoothly along the coast road with the full moon that Lucas had promised her shining above, she gave herself up to the promise of a better understanding between them.

She is so beautiful, he was thinking, and so straightforward. Would she be better off with some local guy as easy to get on with as herself, instead of being caught up in the aftermath of the hurts he'd endured from a man he hadn't known, and a woman that he had trusted? But he loved her and wanted to make her happy. He'd gone into a jeweller's in the town the day before and chosen a ring with sapphires as blue as her eyes and diamonds that sparkled as brightly as Jenna did when she was happy.

Before he'd left The Old Chart House he'd considered whether to take it with him. It would be simple to put it in his pocket and if the opportunity arose ask her to marry him, but that wasn't his way.

His love for Jenna was for life. If she said no when he asked her he would stay on his own for ever, so the asking wasn't going to be a spur-of-the-moment affair with her dubious about his feelings. Tonight was going to be the first step towards the future.

When they arrived the restaurant was filling up, it being Friday night, but a hovering waiter was quick to take them to their table once he knew they had a reservation.

As Lucas seated himself opposite her, Jenna felt like pinching herself to see if she was awake because tonight she wasn't crouched in the window seat hoping for a glimpse of the car moving along the road to Bluebell Cove. He was here in the flesh, watching her with the dark hazel gaze that would hold her heart for ever.

There was a dance floor and when they'd eaten he rose to his feet, took her hand in his and said, 'Are you in the mood?'

'Yes,' she told him laughingly, 'and please take note I'm in all the right colours, no black like that other time.'

'So you haven't forgotten that?'

'Er, no.'

They were on the dance floor now. He was holding out his arms and as she went into them Jenna thought that if this was just a one-off occasion, at least it would be something to remember. Yet she couldn't refrain from asking, 'So, Lucas, what has changed? We don't see each other for ages and then you send me flowers and invite me to dine with you.'

'It might be because since I found you in the kitchen that night I've begun to hope that you don't hate me as much as I imagined you did, and are not as repelled at the thought of me touching you as you were the last time we were on the beach together. Does that answer your question?'

She had stiffened in his arms. 'That was said in hurt and anger. I saw you going back to work at the hospital without telling me as another instance of being kept on the edge of your life, especially as it was my suggestion that you do that.'

'So I gathered, but you were wrong. I'd been working up to telling you all week that I'd decided to take your advice and go back to the hospital, but I was still having my dark moments and was concerned that I might be doing the wrong thing, and if I was, I didn't want you to feel hurt or in any way responsible because you'd suggested it. So I kept putting off telling you until it got to Sunday and I knew I had to do it then or it would be too late.'

'And when you came I wasn't there, was I?' she said as light began to dawn.

'No, you weren't, and I was sickened at my own stupidity. So do we understand each other a little better?'

'Yes, we do. I made too big a thing of it, I suppose, but it did make me feel surplus to requirements.'

His arms had tightened around her and with his lips against her hair he murmured, '*Never that! Never, ever that!'* But she didn't hear him above the music.

When it stopped and they were leaving the dance floor he said, 'Shall we go on to the terrace for a few moments? I love to watch the sea in the moonlight.'

'Yes, so do I, and I love surfing in moonlight even more,' she said, her glance on the dancing waves.

It was a cold night but still, and Jenna thought she would have said yes to going outside if it had been blowing a gale, every second with Lucas was so precious.

'Stay there,' he told her, and went to retrieve her jacket from the cloakroom. As he held it for her to put her arms in she could feel his breath on the back of her neck and resisted the temptation to swivel round so that her mouth would be close to his.

'You know what I wish?' she said softly as they looked down onto age-old rocks bedded into golden sand that was forever welcoming and saying goodbye to the tides.

'What?' he asked, hoping that it was something that would add to the wonder of the moment.

'That we had our surfing equipment with us.'

'You can't be serious!' he exclaimed. 'It's a winter evening, and we're all dressed up.'

'We have facilities for hiring out surfboards and wetsuits,' a member of staff who'd overheard their conversation told them. 'This part of the coast is renowned for some of the best surfing in Devon. There are changing rooms with lockers to keep your belongings safe while you're out there.'

'So?' Jenna said, smiling up at him, eyes bright with anticipation, and he thought the last thing he'd had in mind had been for surfing to be the finale of the evening. Yet it was what they'd been doing when they'd first met and as such the activity would always be special in his life as well as hers if her present enthusiasm was anything to go by.

When they came out of their respective changing rooms ready for action he smiled at the vision they presented and said, 'I thought I was the one prone to doing the unexpected, but this is…'

'Crazy?'

'Mmm, yes.'

'I haven't been in the sea for ages, which is most unusual,' she explained. 'The last time was when I was caught in a rip tide and you dragged me out of it.'

'Maybe the memory of that is why you haven't wanted to surf,' he suggested.

'Yes, that, and one or two other things,' she replied, 'but I can feel the pull of the sea tonight. It must be the thought of surfing in the moonlight.'

'So let's do it!' he cried.

There was always a feeling of exhilaration in surfing, challenging the might of the sea, and this time was no different, except that they were together, in harmony for the first time in weeks, and she wanted the night to go on for ever.

'Was that good?' he asked as they drove back to Bluebell Cove, long past midnight.

She turned to face him in the shadowed light of the car. 'Yes,' she said softly. 'It was all good—the meal, the moonlight, and the surfing, which like life has you in control one moment and the next floundering when the board tips up.'

He was giving her a long thoughtful look and, wishing she hadn't made the comparison, she asked, 'Are you going to be able to relax over the weekend?'

'No chance,' he replied. 'The two operations that were postponed are rescheduled for then. I might take Monday off, though.'

'Have you had any bad moments since you went back?' she asked with the memory of them attending the little girl on the cliffs and George Enderby's heart attack, both occasions when she'd known he'd been under stress and had overcome it.

He smiled. 'Just a couple, but thankfully they soon passed.'

'Have you any regrets?'

'No, I haven't, at least not regarding that, but I do have a regret about something else and we both know what that is.'

'Do we?'

'Yes, don't pretend you don't know what I'm talking about, Jenna.'

'I'm not! It could be a few things, such as you not telling me you were going back to work at the hospital and me having to find out from Ethan. Or you being so adamant that you didn't want to sleep with me when somehow your kisses always suggested that you did, and when, apparently, some other men would be eager to do so given the chance.'

'I'm not other men.'

'Tell me something I don't know already!'

As he was about to reply she put her finger against his lips and said, 'Subject closed, Dr Devereux.'

He laughed. 'You think so, do you, Nurse Balfour? We'll see about that.'

At that moment Four Winds House came into view and Jenna thought that in a few seconds the magical night would be over and she still didn't know if it was a one-off occasion. The only time Lucas had touched her tonight had been when they'd been dancing and that didn't count for much, not when she was melting with longing.

He'd stopped the car at the bottom of the drive and she was holding the door handle ready to get out when he reached across and took both her hands in his. Holding them palms upwards he bent and kissed each one in turn before saying softly, 'Sleep well, golden girl.' Then, releasing them, he went round to the passenger side and held the door while she got out.

When she'd found her door key he walked up the drive with her, and taking it from her he opened the door and said, 'Make sure that you lock it behind you, Jenna.' And as she stood transfixed with disappointment he went back to the car and drove off.

On Monday morning Ethan announced that a report had come through from the hospital regarding the man with shingles who had been rushed to A and E straight from the surgery with severe chest pains.

It said that tests had shown that his pain was due to a build-up of the pain he should have been having from the shingles and hadn't. Where most patients had a lot of discomfort while the blisters were emerging and immediately afterwards, caused by inflammation of the nerve ends, in his case there hadn't been any.

It had been building up instead of coming to the surface and had ended in massive pain that he'd understandably mistaken for a heart attack. Now he was on medication for neuralgia rather than cardiac failure, and making a good recovery.

'So what do you think of that?' he asked Jenna, who had been there when the patient's wife had brought him to the surgery, hoping that Lucas might be available to examine him.

'I think that shingles is a strange illness,' she replied. 'When I was working abroad I once saw a case of it where the pain was acute but there were no blisters and they never did come out, yet it was definitely shingles.'

As the morning progressed she kept remembering that Lucas had said he might have the day free, but each time she glanced across at his house there was no sign of him and she decided that he had either been delayed in Theatre or was having second thoughts after Friday night.

Yet surely he wasn't expecting her to mistake a kiss on the palms of her hands as a binding gesture. She would need more than that to convince her that he loved her as much as she loved him, but there was no time for daydreaming, there were patients to be seen.

There were patients to be seen. Meanwhile, Ethan, looking pale and drawn, had just arrived back from a weekend in France with Francine and the children, and she shuddered at the thought of what was going on in their lives.

With the head of the practice under such stress it was good to have Leo around with his breezy charm that was sometimes at odds with the competence he displayed in his dealings with the patients.

He was still living at Meredith's guest house but had been saying only that morning before surgery that he was house hunting. Bluebell

Cove had cast a spell over him, and all those who'd heard him had understood because it was that sort of place, even in grey December.

Lucas had slept at the hospital on Saturday and Sunday nights in the accommodation provided for staff unable to get home or, as in his case, who needed to be readily available should there be a crisis concerning a patient.

The newborn baby that he'd operated on for a serious heart defect on Saturday might turn out to be one of those, and he'd felt that he owed it to the devastated parents to be there in case anything happened.

The surgery had been a no-choice situation. If it hadn't been performed the tiny one would certainly have died, and having to operate on such a young and premature baby with such a serious diagnosis had been the kind of nightmare he had encountered many times before. Each time it was no less horrendous.

As he'd lain sleepless in the antiseptic atmosphere of the hospital he'd thought about

Jenna and the children he wanted them to have, and silently berated himself for not having already asked her to marry him because she was in his every waking thought, in his blood, in his heart for ever.

He'd been down to see the baby several times during the night and also on Sunday before and after the second of the two operations that had been postponed, and in the grey dawn of Monday morning gave a satisfied nod to the nursing team who had never left his side for a moment since the operation. The little one was breathing more easily, was a better colour, and Lucas thought that maybe later in the day he would be able to return to where his hopes and dreams lay for a while.

The baby's parents, who had been by their newborn's side ever since the operation, were looking a little less tense and he asked them, 'What are you going to call this little fighter of yours?'

The father smiled a tired smile. 'We thought of Lucas.'

'Oh, no!' he said laughingly. 'There are better names than that.'

'We don't think so,' his wife whispered, looking down at her child.

It was the middle of the afternoon when he arrived back in Bluebell Cove, and knowing Jenna would be long gone from the surgery, he showered and changed his clothes before going to find her.

He'd half expected her to have done the same thing as before and been waiting at The Old Chart House to bring cheer to his return, but as she hadn't heard a word from him since they'd separated in the early hours of Saturday morning she was hardly going to have rolled out the red carpet. It was more likely that she'd given up on him, but if he remembered rightly she'd already done that.

As far as she was concerned, she might have decided that Friday night was a one-off and if she had he would have to go back to square one, he thought soberly as he shaved off the stubble that had accumulated over the weekend.

When he reached the headland every other thought was driven from his mind when he saw the orange flash of the lifeboat in the distance, surging across angry waters at full speed.

A crowd had gathered on the beach below and an elderly fisherman told him, 'Two youngsters have been blown out to sea in a dinghy and there's a storm brewin'. It don't look good.'

As Lucas gazed up at a lowering sky he thought it was an understatement. There was grey sky, grey sea, waves as high as a house, and a frail dinghy out there somewhere.

'Jenna Balfour's gone out with the lifeboat,' the old guy went on to say, and Lucas felt the cold hand of dread grip his heart. 'The mother of one of the kids reckons he's got a dicky heart and at the best is never well, so her being a nurse Jenna offered to go along.'

He nodded bleakly. That was what it was all about. He'd done all he could for a helpless baby, now it was Jenna's turn to be there for a couple of kids drifting somewhere out there, and he wasn't going to breathe easily until they were all back on dry land.

When he thought of the ring he'd bought he prayed that he might be given the chance to put it on her finger. The thought of her being out there in such conditions was horrendous. If only he'd got back earlier, he could have gone in her place.

The lifeboat had disappeared and silence had fallen on the crowd. It lasted until they heard the drone of a helicopter in the sky above, indicating that the coastguard station had been on to Air Sea Rescue, and desperate as he was for news Lucas knew he had to look after Barbara and Keith. Her heart was not as good as it might have been, far from it, and if they knew what was going on out there it could trigger an attack.

When Keith opened the door to him he was pale and shaken and told him, 'I'm worried sick about Jenna and those boys, but Barbara is cool as a cucumber. You'll find her in the sitting room.'

She was as he'd said when Lucas found her, and he didn't know whether to feel angry or sad at the extent of her calmness.

She smiled and it was as wintry as the weather outside. 'She's *my* daughter, Lucas,' she told him, 'and so I know she will cope. I've done what Jenna is doing a few times over the years and it is no picnic, believe me.

'But it is what we're paid for, what we're here to do on this planet, save the sick and suffering. You might not think it, but I am proud of her, so very proud. So do go back to the beach and don't come back until you have our girl with you, as you're the first person she'll want to see.'

'I'm not sure about that,' he said grimly.

'You should be. Jenna loves you very much.'

'Has she said so?'

'No, she doesn't need to. If you're not sure, ask her.'

'I've got to get her back first and at this moment that is all that matters. Whether she loves me or not can come later,' he told her, and with an urgency inside him to a degree that he would never have believed possible he went striding down amongst the rocks on the cliff side, all the time scanning the ocean for the return of the lifeboat and its occupants.

The light was fading. The winter afternoon had run its course when a shout went up amongst those waiting on the beach. The noise of the helicopter could be heard in the low clouds above them and on the horizon the lifeboat was ploughing its way through the rampant sea.

Knowing that it would go straight to the harbour where it was housed, there was a general exodus in that direction, with Lucas slowing down to let the car with the parents of the two boys in it speed past.

Jenna was there on the quayside with her hair hanging limply around a face blue with cold when he arrived, and joy bells rang in his heart. She was safe. When he got to her she was helping in the transfer of the two lost boys into a waiting ambulance while paramedics were wrapping them in space blankets to bring up their body heat and giving one of them oxygen.

When it pulled away with their parents beside

them he handed her his phone and said softly, 'Ring your parents, Jenna, to let them know that everyone is safe, including yourself, and then I'll drive you to my place, where you can dry out and get warm again.'

She shook her head. 'One of the boys is said to have a heart problem and they're both in shock and very cold,' she said anxiously. 'Can we follow the ambulance? I need to be sure they're going to be all right. It was touch and go, you know, they were clinging onto the dinghy for dear life.'

'Yes, of course,' he said. 'I'll take a look at the one with the heart trouble myself if need be.'

'I love you for that,' she said softly. 'What time did you arrive back from the hospital?'

'About the same time that I discovered you were out there in the lifeboat.'

She was stripping off the protective clothing that the lifeboat crew had kitted her out in before they'd set off on their rescue mission, and when she was free of it and had handed it back he said, 'So let's be moving, and when we get there I'll show you the tiny scrap that I operated on Saturday night. It was a life-and-death affair of a newborn with a heart defect and thankfully when I left earlier this afternoon the little one was still holding onto life.'

They were driving along the main highway into the town now and as what he was saying sank in she said, 'So you've been working all over the weekend. Didn't you come home to sleep?'

'I could have done, but stayed at the hospital as I thought I might be needed during the night. As it happened, I wasn't, but I was up and down all the time, checking on my small patient and trying to provide reassurance to his parents.'

'And now I'm dragging you back there,' she said apologetically.

He flashed her a smile that was so tender she felt herself go weak at the message it was conveying, and then throwing her into even more chaos he said, 'You can drag me anywhere you like. Just to have you safe beside me is all I ask at this moment.'

It was true, but before this eventful day had run its course there was something he still had to do—connected with a certain ring.

CHAPTER TEN

THE two boys were still very shaken when Jenna and Lucas saw them at the hospital, and treatment for hypothermia was being continued in the form of hot baths and warm drinks.

'I believe that your son has a heart problem,' Lucas said to the parents of the boy whose mother had mentioned it when the alarm had been raised. 'What exactly is it? I'm a heart surgeon, so it is of interest to me.'

Before his wife could reply, the father said, 'Thomas had suspected rheumatic fever when he was small and the doctor told us it could leave him with something called myocarditis, which affects the heart valves.

'But when they tested him for it he hadn't got anything like that and it was never very clear if he'd actually had rheumatic fever, but ever since then his mother has been convinced that he has something wrong with his heart and mollycoddles him all the time.'

As his wife snorted indignantly Lucas said, 'Why not make an appointment for me to see him and we'll settle the matter once and for all? If there is anything wrong we can get it seen to, and if there isn't you will be able to put any further anxiety from your minds.'

'That would be great,' the man said, and turned to his wife. 'Wouldn't it, Marge?'

'Yes, it would,' she agreed, and added, still indignant, 'Not that *you've* ever lost any sleep over it.'

Satisfied that the two boys seemed to be recovering all right from their ordeal, they left the ward and once in the corridor outside Jenna said, 'I am so sorry that I got you involved in that. I wonder if Thomas's parents know how fortunate they are to be given the chance to see someone like you without even having to wait in the queue.'

'I'll see them at home if they get in touch. I don't want to breach any hospital rules or jump any waiting lists, and now do you want to see the baby I told you about? I need to check his progress.'

'Of course I do,' she said immediately. 'Lead me to him.'

When they appeared, the nurse who had been watching over him disappeared tactfully, and when Jenna looked down at the tiny infant that Lucas had brought back from the brink, she said softly, 'Oh! Poor little mite! What was it?'

'Septal defect, hole in the heart.'

'He's beautiful!'

'He will be when we can remove some of the tubes,' he volunteered, and looked around him. 'It seems as if the parents might be having a break. They've never moved from his side since the moment he was born and they were told there was a problem, a big one.'

He was reaching for the baby's notes on the clipboard at the bottom of the bed and when he'd finished reading them he asked casually, 'Do you want children, Jenna?'

She stared at him blankly. 'Yes, of course I do.' Wanting to know what had prompted the question, she came up with one of her own. 'Don't you?'

'Oh, yes,' he said in a low voice. 'I want a family of my own more than words can say,' and thought, *But only with you as their mother.*

The nurse was hovering and when he'd satisfied himself that all was well with his small patient he told her, 'I'll be in to see him again tomorrow, Nurse, and in the meantime I want to know about even the slightest problem should any arise. I don't want any setbacks if they can be avoided.' She nodded obediently and they left the sleeping child in her care.

'Now, can I take you home?' he asked as they left the hospital. 'I'm sure that your parents would like to see for themselves that you're safe. Your father was distraught when you'd gone with the lifeboat, but your mother was taking it all in her stride. Told me it was something that she'd had to do a few times in the past and that as her daughter she had no worries about whether you would be able to cope.'

'Really! What could I have done to deserve that?'

'She loves you in her own way, Jenna. And she respects you.'

'Yes, I suppose she does,' she agreed, 'but it would choke her to say so.'

Was she thinking that he would be the same? he thought. Little did she know that if it hadn't been for the storm and the trauma of the lost boys he had been going to ask her to marry him today. But he could tell she was exhausted, would be upset if he asked her something so important to them both when she was too tired to embrace the moment.

'Sleep well,' he told her when he dropped her off.

'Aren't you going to come in for a moment?' she asked disappointedly.

'No, you're tired. I'll be in touch tomorrow. And, Jenna...'

'What?'

'I'll be at Hunters Hill again in the morning and will check on those lads for you, so don't rush off there the moment you've finished at the practice.'

'All right, I'll remember what you've said, but before you go tell me one thing, Lucas. What would you have done if I hadn't come back out of the storm?'

'Gone into a monastery,' he said whimsically. 'So you see what you've saved me from.' And before she could reply the car was on the move and he was waving goodbye.

He would have gone insane if she'd perished out there in the roughest sea he'd ever seen, Lucas was thinking sombrely as he drove up the hill to the village. So why hadn't he told her that instead of making light of it? On impulse he turned the car round and drove back to Four Winds House and when she opened the door said, 'That was a stupid thing to say. Forgive me.'

As she observed him wide-eyed, he reached out and kissed her, just once and fleetingly, but it was the same as before, like a dream becoming reality.

Then once again he was gone and she went back inside, sank down onto the nearest chair and wondered if she would ever understand the workings of his mind.

She understood the workings of her own only too well and when he'd asked her if she wanted children it would have been so easy to say, *Yes, but only if they're yours.* But she'd been down that road once, been too eager, and the next time, if there ever was one, Lucas would have to do the asking.

He rang her at the surgery in the middle of the next morning to tell her that the two youngsters were being discharged later in the day and to say that Thomas's parents hadn't forgotten the offer he'd made the day before.

'As if they would!' she exclaimed. 'Let's hope that you can give his mother peace of mind, and that if there is a problem his father will be able to adjust to the fact. And how is the little poorly one this morning? Has he got a name, by the way?'

'He is still improving, I'm pleased to say, and

his parents are insisting on calling him Lucas, which is embarrassing. It's happened before and will probably happen again, but I wish they wouldn't. There are much nicer names.'

'Not many,' she protested. Her voice softened. 'That is lovely, Lucas.'

'Yes, I suppose so,' he agreed, 'and now, before I have Ethan after me for taking you away from your patients, how are you, Jenna? Have you recovered from yesterday?'

'From what?' she teased. 'The elements or your unexpected return?'

'Er, the elements, of course. Me coming back was just a matter of expressing my concern.'

'Oh, I see,' she said flatly. 'I'm glad you've told me, and now I have to go as Ethan is rather frayed this morning. He's upset because he says it should have been him going out in the lifeboat in that ghastly weather, but as I keep telling him he couldn't have been in two places at once. He was in Plymouth at a meeting when the storm blew up.'

'OK,' he said easily. 'He's fraught enough at the

moment, but just tell me one thing before you go—do they still serve cream teas around here at this time of the year?'

'Yes. Maybe not at so many places as in the summer, but they serve them at the hotel with the thatched roof that we went to that night.'

'So, I'll pick you up at half-past four if that's all right with you. I have a reasonably quiet day in front of me, so I should be free by then.'

'Why?'

'Why have I got a quiet day?'

'No. Why do you want to take me out? You've already expressed your concern on my behalf last night. You don't have to finish it off with a cream tea.'

'Just be ready, will you?' he said equably, as if speaking to a fractious child, and rang off.

The Mercedes pulled up at the front of the house at exactly half-past four in the dark winter afternoon and Jenna thought, This is farcical, going for a cream tea on such a day.

But she got into the car and threw him a pale

smile as he said laughingly, 'I was expecting you to have the black on in keeping with your sombre manner this morning, but I see you must have perked up.'

She was wearing a heavy knit winter suit of fine sapphire blue wool with a pale cream top and matching bag, and after the salt spray of the day before her hair hung clean and shining around the face that filled his every waking thought.

What he was going to do if she refused when he asked her to marry him didn't bear thinking about. But he just couldn't wait any longer. If after all these weeks Jenna still thought it was because he was on the rebound from his broken engagement to Philippa, he would not know where to turn next.

He'd booked a table at the hotel and after she'd seated herself he asked to be excused and went to speak to one of the waiters. While he was gone she looked around her, taking in the fact that the place was half-empty and thinking it wasn't surprising in the depths of winter. She picked up the menu and at the same time Lucas came back to join her.

When she glanced up enquiringly he said smoothly, 'I was asking them to let us know if there are any weather warnings while we're dining as there have been a few today and I don't want us to be stranded out here in the wilds.'

She looked around her and thought that he had a point, but why had they come here instead of going somewhere local? Maybe it was because it was the first place they'd been to together and in the middle of summer the Devonshire countryside had been at its most attractive, but it wasn't the same today. It was, however, very cosy inside, with a big log fire burning in the grate.

They'd placed their order and were waiting for the food to be served. The few tables that had been occupied were now empty and it felt odd, just the two of them in the deserted restaurant, yet she could hear voices coming from somewhere nearby.

A waiter appeared, pushing a serving trolley towards their table, and on it was the wine they'd ordered and a small silver salver covered by a white napkin. He was smiling and bowed to each of them in turn and Jenna thought that he must be giving them the big welcome because they were the only customers present.

When the waiter poured a little of the wine for Lucas to taste and he'd expressed his approval, they were left alone. As they raised their glasses Lucas said softly, 'To us, Jenna,' and removed the napkin to reveal the circle of sapphires and diamonds that he had been longing to place on her finger.

He picked it up, watching the colour drain from her face as he did so, and said, 'Will you marry me, Jenna?' As the pink came flooding back into her cheeks he reminded her gently, 'I did say that I would do the asking when the time came, didn't I?'

'Yes, you did,' she breathed, 'and the answer is yes. I've wanted you from the moment we met, when we almost collided on the beach that day. It was just sexual chemistry at first, but before long I knew that you were the only man I would ever love. I've prayed that one day you would say the words that you've just said, and, Lucas, you shall have the family that you long for, God willing.'

The next few moments were a blur as he slipped the ring onto her finger, took her in his arms and kissed her until she was breathless with the joy of it, and when finally they drew apart her eyes widened.

The restaurant was empty no more. While she'd been engrossed in her future husband it had filled up, filled up with those who cared about her and that she cared for in return.

Her mother was there, dabbing her eyes, with her father seated nearby. Lucy and young Maria were not far away, and there was Ronnie with the rest of his family. Ethan had just appeared and amazingly had his children Kirstie and Ben with him, and Leo was there, chatting to Jack Enderby, of all people, and his father George.

As she surveyed them all she cried laughingly, 'What would all of you have done if I'd said no?'

'Disowned you,' her mother said with the kind of dry humour that was her style, and her father smiled across at his daughter with all his love for her clear to see.

'What would I have done if you'd said no?' Lucas murmured, with his arms around her. 'I know I kept you at a distance, but I was so afraid you might think I was simply on the rebound from what happened before.'

Ethan was on his feet and silence fell on the gathered company as he began to speak.

'We all know that if there is one thing that the people in Bluebell Cove like it's a wedding, especially a Christmas wedding.' He turned to Jenna and Lucas. 'How would you both feel about that? Could you be ready in time?'

'There are still a few weeks to go,' Jenna said thoughtfully. 'I'd love a Christmas wedding, but these days venues for receptions are in so much demand some are booked up years in advance, so that creates a problem straight away.'

'Not if you have it at our place,' Jack Enderby said. 'You can have the big room that we use for the ball.' He glanced at his father. 'One good turn deserves another. And I'm sure that the firm who caters for the ball will sort you out if you tell them that the Enderbys have recommended them.'

'Yes, oh, yes, please!' she cried, and Lucas thought these people would be his people from now on, the same as they were hers. He would be blessed in every way, but most of all because Jenna was going to marry him.

The days were passing and the wedding plans taking shape. Jenna and her mother, with Kirstie, who was to be bridesmaid, and Lucy tagging along for support, had been to a wedding boutique in the town.

There Jenna had chosen a dress that all of them thought was perfect. It was white lace with a tight-fitting bodice, three-quarter sleeves, and a long train that her young attendant would hold as she walked up the aisle with her father.

For Kirstie, who was dark-eyed and dark-haired, it was a pretty pink dress with lots of twirls in it, and as the two older women had observed the bride and her bridesmaid in their dresses it had been handkerchiefs out, even for Barbara.

Ethan's children were in Bluebell Cove on an extended stay to include Christmas. Their mother had agreed to it, but had refused to come herself. He was so happy to have them home he was on cloud nine, or would have been if Francine had wanted to come with them.

But as it was, he didn't intend letting it spoil their time together and had been delighted when Jenna had asked if Kirstie could be her bridesmaid. He had arranged for them to attend local schools again while they were over and after the first few days of adjustment they'd settled in happily.

The wedding was to take place on the day of Christmas Eve. The caterers had agreed to provide the food for the wedding meal in the afternoon and for the evening buffet, which was relieving the festivities committee of the task of catering after the dancing between the two Christmas trees.

It had been arranged that the newlyweds would lead the long line of dancers through the village for the kind of event that would be wonderful if it was a fine night and not too cold, and a catastrophe if it wasn't. But the idea had gripped everyone's imagination and, hail, rain or snow, they were not to be put off.

For Jenna the days of waiting were filled with wonder. Soon they would be together in the house that Lucas had made so attractive after years of neglect. When the alterations had been finished and a consultancy for private patients created, he was going to take two afternoons away from the hospital each week to see them, and Jenna would be his assistant as she'd been before.

There was joy in knowing that they would still be in Bluebell Cove with the surgery nearby and her mother and father not far away in the house on the headland, near enough if they needed her, and with Lucas adoring her every moment they were together, and even when they were apart, her happiness was complete.

Lucas's tiny namesake was home at last and gradually making up for lost time, and Thomas with the laid-back father and over-fussy mother had been seen by Lucas and had tests that had shown he was free from any heart defect, which had brought a smug smile to his father's face and relief to his mother's.

On a Sunday afternoon in the middle of December Jenna and Lucas went with a crowd of others to the beach to watch the nativity play that was being performed that afternoon while the tide was out, and they exchanged smiles when Ethan's son Ben appeared, leading one of the donkeys that was usually occupied in giving children rides.

A girl of a similar age was seated on it dressed in blue with a doll in her arms, and as they moved along slowly until they came to a big rock that had been dressed up to look like an inn, Jenna thought affectionately that young Ben was getting his turn to be on view. He'd scorned being a page-boy at the wedding but wasn't averse to taking part in the play, and she wished that Francine might have been there to see him.

When Jenna awoke on the morning of the twenty-fourth of December her first thoughts were that it was her wedding day and that the night just gone was the last time she would sleep in that room.

No more would she crouch on the window seat for a glimpse of Lucas driving along the coast road. For the rest of her life he would be there beside her when she awoke and it would be heaven on earth.

It was a cold, clear morning with blue skies above and a faint breeze blowing in from the sea. Would it stay that way, she wondered, for the most important day of her life? Snow had been forecast and it was cold enough for it, but so far there was no sign, which was a shame as a white wedding in a snow-covered village would be so beautiful.

But there were things to do before the wedding, like helping her mother to get dressed, and holding her father close on her last day of living in Four Winds House.

She would be around for them both all of the time, but after today she would belong to Lucas, and part of the happiness that it brought would be because her parents were so delighted for her. And if some of her mother's approval came from her daughter marrying a heart surgeon, what did it matter?

To her, Jenna, he was simply the man she loved more than words could express, and she was going to spend the rest of her life making him happy.

When she arrived at the church on her father's arm the incredible was happening. Snow was falling and already a white carpet was forming at their feet. It was going to make her perfect day even more perfect, she thought joyfully, and when she stood in the open doorway and the sound of the wedding march rang up into the rafters, the tall figure waiting at the altar with Ethan by his side turned, and as their glances met she knew that for ever and always he would be hers.

It was evening and as was often the case after a snowfall it was warmer, and as those with dancing feet assembled in the square, the snow now lay thick and white on the ground.

Taking his new wife, who was still in her wedding dress, into his arms, Lucas said, 'May I have this dance, Mrs Devereux?'

At that moment the village school's band began to play and they began to dance a sedate waltz instead of the brisk polka that had been planned before the snow had fallen, and as the tree on the headland came into her line of sight and the lights of a ship out at sea twinkled across the water Jenna said, 'Everything I love is here, Lucas. The sea, the sand, my old home with my parents in it, the village just behind us, *and you, the one I love most of all.'*

It was the end of the most wonderful day of his life, Lucas thought as he stood by the bedroom window, looking out onto the winter wonderland that had graced his wedding day.

He was waiting for Jenna to come to him and suddenly she was there, standing before him, more beautiful than he could ever have imagined, and as his senses leapt and his heart rejoiced he hadn't forgotten that he'd said he would do the asking and he said softly, 'When we've made love will you want to sleep in my bed with me, Jenna?' He pointed to the jagged scar that ran across his chest. 'Next to this?'

She was reaching out for him, gently caressing the reminder of one of the worst days of his life, and as he gazed down at her she said tenderly, 'Yes, of course I will, Lucas. I will consider it a privilege. I've wanted to hold you close ever since I first saw it.'

MEDICAL™

Large Print

Titles for the next three months...

December

THE MIDWIFE AND THE MILLIONAIRE	Fiona McArthur
FROM SINGLE MUM TO LADY	Judy Campbell
KNIGHT ON THE CHILDREN'S WARD	Carol Marinelli
CHILDREN'S DOCTOR, SHY NURSE	Molly Evans
HAWAIIAN SUNSET, DREAM PROPOSAL	Joanna Neil
RESCUED: MOTHER AND BABY	Anne Fraser

January

DARE SHE DATE THE DREAMY DOC?	Sarah Morgan
DR DROP-DEAD GORGEOUS	Emily Forbes
HER BROODING ITALIAN SURGEON	Fiona Lowe
A FATHER FOR BABY ROSE	Margaret Barker
NEUROSURGEON...AND MUM!	Kate Hardy
WEDDING IN DARLING DOWNS	Leah Martyn

February

WISHING FOR A MIRACLE	Alison Roberts
THE MARRY-ME WISH	Alison Roberts
PRINCE CHARMING OF HARLEY STREET	Anne Fraser
THE HEART DOCTOR AND THE BABY	Lynne Marshall
THE SECRET DOCTOR	Joanna Neil
THE DOCTOR'S DOUBLE TROUBLE	Lucy Clark

⊚™ MILLS & BOON®